little blue lies

CHRIS LYNCH

little blue lies

SIMON & SCHUSTER BFYR

New York   London   Toronto   Sydney   New Delhi

SIMON & SCHUSTER BFYR

An imprint of Simon & Schuster Children's Publishing Division
1230 Avenue of the Americas, New York, New York 10020
This book is a work of fiction. Any references to historical events, real people, or real places are used fictitiously. Other names, characters, places, and events are products of the author's imagination, and any resemblance to actual events or places or persons, living or dead, is entirely coincidental.
SIMON & SCHUSTER BFYR is a trademark of Simon & Schuster, Inc.
For information about special discounts for bulk purchases,
please contact Simon & Schuster Special Sales at 1-866-506-1949
or business@simonandschuster.com.
The Simon & Schuster Speakers Bureau can bring authors to your live event.
For more information or to book an event, contact
the Simon & Schuster Speakers Bureau at 1-866-248-3049
or visit our website at www.simonspeakers.com.
Jacket design and illustration by Krista Vossen
Interior design by Hilary Zarycky
The text for this book is set in Berling.
Manufactured in the United States of America
2 4 6 8 10 9 7 5 3 1
Library of Congress Cataloging-in-Publication Data
Lynch, Chris, 1962–
Little blue lies / Chris Lynch. — 1st ed.
p. cm.
Summary: Oliver, known as "O," and his suddenly ex-girlfriend Junie are are known for telling little lies, but one of Junie's lies about not winning the lottery could get her into trouble with a local mob boss.
ISBN 978-1-4424-4008-1 (hardcover : alk. paper)
ISBN 978-1-4424-4010-4 (eBook)
[1. Honesty—Fiction. 2. Dating (Social customs)—Fiction.
3. Organized crime—Fiction.] I. Title.
PZ7.L979739Lit 2014
[Fic]—dc23
2012041877

FIRST
EDITION

To my lovely wifeling, Julie Blue Eyes

One

The problem, or thrill, depending on how you choose to look at it, was that our relationship was practically *based* on an enthusiastic mendacity. Her nickname for me was Lyin' O'Brien. Mine for her was Sweet Junie Blue Lies.

She told me in one of our earliest conversations that her mother had died in a plane crash. And that she had an airplane tattooed on her hip with her mother's initials on the wings. Then I ran into her at CVS four weeks later, where I was cheerfully introduced to her living, earth-walking mother, as well as her sister, Max, who I had been led to believe was her brother, Max. Oh, not an actual plane crash, she said. That was just a metaphor for the marriage. Then after another six long weeks I finally met Junie's hip. There was, in fact, an airplane tattoo. The origin of the initials changed every time I asked. I stopped asking.

Still, thrill is how I choose to look at it. She made lying exciting, and sporty, and really I picked up the habit only when she got me hooked. It was our bond. Then again, we're not together anymore either, so my assessment could be open to question.

June Blue. A guy does not break up with that name lightly. Or voluntarily, as it happens. I was dumped.

She says that her grandfather is a rabbi in London, and I have no reason to doubt her. I told her my grandfather was a bishop in Waterford, and I have no reason not to believe me, either. I've been to his grave, and his headstone is shaped like one of those hats. There you go.

Right? So if that's not soul-matey enough for you, there's our fathers. No, not "Our Fathers," like that moan prayer they used to push in the church, and which would not ever have crossed Junie Blue's puffy orange lips. Our actual fathers. Mine is a robber baron and hers is—whatcha know?—the regular kind. And don't go thinking I mean "baron," all right, since what in the world would a *regular* baron be like?

And they both sell, among other things, insurance.

Before I met him, she told me her father looked exactly like John F. Kennedy. Then I met him. If you dug Kennedy up today, he'd still be better-looking.

Yet in spite of all that, June and I are as honest as the day is long. Unless you count lying, which, really, nobody does.

Honest day's work/honest day's pay, we have no quarrel with that business at all. She works two jobs too, one having grown out of the other, and both legitimate. She works evening and early morning and weekend hours at the corner-store that is about seven corners away from her house. It's in a neighborhood where all corner-store counters would be bulletproof Plexiglassed from the criminals, but for the fact that all their criminals are *their* criminals. And all of *those* criminals are operating under the benevolent eye of One Who Knows, who does not like his neighborhood being dirtied up by petty crime and unwholesomeness that detracts from his sepia view of life in the microclimate that extends four miles in every direction from his modest not-quite-beachside house. You wind up with kneecap and testicle troubles if you screw with One Who Knows and the sepia view.

Junie's humor, right? It's like this. Everybody knows One Who Knows as One Who Knows, except, when we would talk about him, it bothered her to have to sound so, you know, reverential to the guy. Even though she has met him on many occasions and likes him fine enough, she's got her principles still. The guy even has the tattoo down one forearm, the initials stacked like a totem pole, *OWK*. "Owk," Junie said one day, calling me from the store just after he left. He bought a loaf of Wonder Bread and a whole roll of scratch cards and as usual tipped her with ten of those cards. "I mean, thanks for the cards, *Owk*, but, really, *Owk*? It's not even a word or a decent acronym or anything. It's like you asked an owl, 'Hey, what kinda bird are you,' and just when he goes to tell you,

you punch him in the stomach. That's the noise he would make, '*Owk!*'"

I laughed, like I did almost all the time when she talked, but then, also like usual, I began the reasoning process. "So, nobody asked you to call him that. Just use his proper name. One Who Knows."

"Aw, shit to that. I'm not calling anybody that."

"Why not? It's got a ring. Listen," I said, and ran through the full phrasing several different ways, slow and fast and articulated and mumbled and—

"Hold it," she said.

"What?"

"That last one. Do that last one again."

"As I recall," I said, "it went a little something like this . . ."

"That's it," she said.

What I did was rush the three words together, with an opening flourish and a gentle fade-out at the end. Nice work, but nothing special. I do stuff like that all the time.

"Juan Junose." She said the *J*s making *H* sounds, and I could hear her smiling. She has big pearly teeth with a middle gap you could park a cigarette in, which she does sometimes, and it's heart-flutter stuff. Smoking and hearts, eh?

"Juan?" I said.

"From this point onward. Or, Juanward."

I loved the Spanishness of it. Particularly as our Mr.

Junose is the type of guy who, if he found himself being any kind of Spanish, he'd shoot himself in the face.

"Juan," we said at the same time and in the same key. Soul-matey, right?

We did stuff like that regularly, at least until school finished and we unfortunately did likewise. We graduated a month ago, and everything was sailing along like a happy horny boat like always until we hit the reef. I never saw it coming.

"Why?" I asked, and the only reason I didn't sound like a complete weenie dog was because I was taken so entirely by surprise. Given even just a little bit of advance notice, I would have worked up a whimper that would still be singing today if you walked down to the beach and put a seashell to your ear.

I liked June Blue very much. Still do.

"Because we're not kids anymore, O." She liked to call me O, because it fit so well into most of our conversations. *O, for Christsake . . . O, shut up . . . O, God, put that thing away. There are kids in the park. . . .*

"Yes, we are," I said. "Don't let that graduation thing fool you. We're still kids, and will be for quite some time."

She just shook her head at me sadly from her spot so far away at the other end of the seesaw.

"Your head's going in the wrong direction," I said, suddenly bumping the seesaw up and down frantically, getting her whole self into the proper nodding action.

She giggled gloriously but didn't change her mind. She held fast to the seesaw and to the horrible sad squint that was maiming her features. Confusion and panic ran through me like a fast-acting poison, and so, being a clever guy and quick on my feet, I did something.

See, probably the one bone of contention we ever had in a year and a half of going out was that my folks have money, and so I have money, and her family doesn't have anything like that. A problem for her, but I was always cool and magnanimous with it.

So I did something.

"No," she said. "No. You did not."

"What?" I said, removing my hands from the seesaw so I could make the ineffective pleading gesture to the heavens.

"You did *not* just offer me money to stay with you."

Pleading hands were required to stay where they were. "What? No. It wasn't . . . That's not . . . You just misconstrued . . ."

We had the balance thing going pretty well, considering that I outweigh her by about thirty pounds, but when she flung herself backward to get off the seesaw and out of my life, I dropped like a pre-fledgling baby bird to the ground.

And if one of those nestless, flightless, awkward bundles

of patchy feather and hollow bone had been blown up to adult human size and plunked on the ground at the down end of a seesaw, he would not have looked one chirp more ludicrous than I did at that moment.

But I didn't care about that.

"Junie?" I called desperately.

"If you even dare try to follow me, I'll have your legs broken, O."

And since June Blue is one of those rare people who can say that and actually do that and can do it on speed dial, I just sat with my bruised everything until two seesaw-deprived preschool girls came along and stared me into slouching away home.

Her second job is dog walker. Visitors to the store started asking after she took care of the owner's mutt for a couple of days when he had a couple of toes excommunicated because of diabetes. People in June's neighborhood apparently have diabetes at such a rate that people get toes popped like having bad teeth removed, and word spreads fast when there is a reliable babysitter, window washer, or dog walker around. June is popular, and busy, and one of her sometimes clients is the man himself, Juan, who has the ugliest Boston terrier on earth, with three deep scars across his snout and an ass like a tiny little baboon.

I take walks sometimes. It's not stalking.

I don't take binoculars, or rope, or flowers.

I take hope, best intentions, and, okay, that spicy ginger chewing gum that she loves and you can only get in Chinatown, but that hardly changes anything.

"That tree isn't even wider than you, doofus," she says.

What does one do in this situation? I'm looking a little simple here, skinnying myself behind this immature beech tree diagonally across from the house that June has just stepped out of. I'm not stupid. I know this tree is not adequate for my purpose, but I had my eye on a burly elm only fifteen yards farther, when June and that Airedale with the bad nature stepped out the door a full ten minutes before the usual walking time for a Tuesday.

"I'm not stalking you," I say, still inexplicably remaining there, only partially obscured by the sapling. I may have lost my fastball, lying-wise.

She continues on her appointed round.

"Stalking Archie, then?"

"He's not my type."

"Good. 'Cause he doesn't like you either."

It's true, he doesn't, but more important, what did she mean by that, "doesn't like you, either"? *Either* as in, Archie and I share a mutual animosity? Or she and Archie share a dislike of me? This is the kind of stupid, obsessive thought

I have now? Look what you've done to me, Junie Blue.

"Did you just say you didn't like me?" I say pathetically as she strides down the block and away from me again.

"No," she says. And that's all she says.

"Gum?" I call after her, the pack held aloft like I am the Statue of Liberty's tiny little embarrassing brother.

The high school we went to is often cited in lists as America's finest public school. There is a citywide exam to get in after sixth grade, and I was determined to take it even though the highly rated private school I went to had everything but its own moat. I alarmed my parents both by doing well on the exam and by insisting on going there. Rebellion? No. I'm pretty sure I was intent on meeting a greater variety of girl-folk. There were no Junie Blues in my previous existence, that's for sure.

When June and I were still students there, things were much better. We had two classes together final term, and I tell you what, in those classes I did not learn a money-humping thing.

English and history, and we clung like mutual barnacles to each other's hull for every class, making jokes and talking all manner of nonsense. We had our regular seats, and we would always make plans to meet there, as if there were any mystery at all as to where we were going to sit.

"Back of English," she would say, pointing at me as we

passed in the corridor prior to third period Tuesday and Thursday.

"Wrong side of history," I would say prior to fourth period Wednesday and Friday. It was a favorite term of our history teacher, Mr. Lyons, whom everybody called Jake, and who talked with this fantastic squelch effect like he had a tracheotomy. *You don't want to wind up on the wrong side of history*, Jake would say whenever he was pointing out some of the greatest errors in judgment that hindsight could illuminate. I always thought hindsight gave history teachers the most lopsided advantage over pretty much everybody they ever talked about, but Jake was rather modest in his infallibility just the same.

In more practical terms the wrong side of our history was in the southwest corner of the room, where the window was drafty and the overhead light flickered like in a disco. I sat behind June and rubbed her shoulders when the wind blew, and that buzzing overhead fluorescent was a kind of sound track to our little wrong-side romance. Bzzzz.

The point, though, was that the back of English, the wrong side of history, wherever we were in May was a better place than where we were just a few weeks later, and I am none the wiser still as to why.

Bad overhead lighting makes me melancholy now.

Two

My mother is a freelance graphic artist, which means she works most of the time at home, which means the house is almost never mine. She does sketches of me from time to time, and of course they are technically very good, but in every single portrait I look like I'm trying to sell you something.

My father runs his own financial services business. He is always trying to sell you something.

I have the summer off, courtesy of my indulgent parents, to figure out just what I want to do with—

Wait. She's lying. Of course. How stupid of me. Of course she's lying. That's what she does, my Sweet Junie Blue Lies. That's what *we* do. She didn't dump me; she teased and provoked and tested me. It was like a grand graduation present, and I screwed it up completely by failing for all these weeks to recognize it.

I am not even worthy of the title Lyin' O'Brien. I am deeply ashamed.

It is with great relief and excitement that I text her: *I get it. You almost had me there, ya Blue Lying Minx. Can I come over now and make up for lost time?*

I sit back up against my headboard, dreaming like I used to dream, of Junie and me and all the better things. It's so great because it's a Friday and everything. Not too big a man to admit that I check my phone every four seconds or so, to see if I have my response. After twenty-four seconds or so the tension mounts, but then, bam, it's in.

It is not the response I expected.

Shitty timing, it says.

What timing? I've given her forever.

Come on, June, this is stupid. Can't we stop it?

I sit on my bed some more and I wait for June to come to her senses. I think of several hundred more texts to add, to tip this thing in the right direction, texts about how we don't want to be caught on the wrong side of history, and changing my name to Cryin' O'Brien now, the kind of knockout material that cannot fail to tickle that Junie Blue spot that only I know about. But I hold back, not to be cool exactly, since there is nothing she would see through more quickly than me trying to be cool with her, but to keep something in reserve, to keep my powder dry for the all-out assault that may be necessary.

I wait, trying to pretend I'm not waiting, until waiting becomes not unlike plunging my whole head into a vat of icy sparkling water and keeping my eyes open to count all the bubbles rushing at me. I am aware of shifting positions on the bed, twisting this way and that, with my phone on the night table as if it can be made aware that I am ignoring it and thereby provoked into ringing.

Knock, knock.

"Who's there?"

This is neither a knock-knock joke nor a real question, since we know this is my mother at the door. She works, like I said, at home, which sucks sometimes, and she has ears like a bat. She's kind of obsessive about something I'm not thrilled to talk about, but suffice it to say my *tossing and turning* just now provoked her into action. Somewhere along the line she got the idea that this summer I'm jerking myself to the point of hairy-handed criminal insanity, and so, by golly, as long as she is in the house, monkeys will not be spanked. Nor will there be any snapping the squid, flogging the dolphin, whacking the haddock, pulling the python, choking the chicken, or clubbing the baby seal. She's the World Wildlife Fund of self-pleasure.

Usually the ruse is a snack of some kind.

"It's me."

"Hi, Mom. I'm a little busy right now."

"I have tuna on toast and kettle chips, and bread-and-butter pickle slices," she snaps, with such urgency that I expect to see the indentation of her face present itself in the door.

"Thanks," I say, "but I'll—"

The phone beeps me off midsentence. I scramble across the bed to get it.

"Hello?" Mom says, a bit exasperated.

I grunt nonwords at her as I retrieve the text.

"Arggh," she says, storming away.

"Sorry," I say. I was rude. Though not as rude as she thinks.

Come over right now right now, is what the text tells me to do.

Right now right now my feet are on the floor, through the door, and down the stairs, and I hear my mother crow something in my direction, but I have no time for that as I slam the big oak front door behind me, and because of a light rain falling and coating the pavement, I pretty well hydroplane all the way over to Junie's place with "stupid" surely smeared all over my face.

I have to say. I have to say. I think I like Junie Blue even more than I thought I did, and I am undecided about whether to tell her that.

As I turn the final slick corner onto June's street—rain always seems to rain rainier on her neighborhood than mine—I lose my legs. My feet shoot sideways in the slickness, and my whole self follows, until I feel like I'm sliding safely into third. In fact I am sliding unsafely right off the sidewalk and into light traffic that screeches and beeps. Somebody screams terror and somebody else laughs and cheers, until me and a four-wheeler monstrosity skitter to a halt about three feet before death. Mine, most likely.

I am staring straight up into a wheel well when the lady who was driving comes running over to where I am, crying wildly—her—as if I am for sure already dead and murdering her insurance premium situation.

She stares down at me with her hands covering her mouth, but they don't filter out any of the blubbering. "Aww-wwww," she says.

"You've got some rust starting under here," I say, so unbelievably composed that I fall instantly in love with myself and curse the fact that Junie Blue is not right here to see it. Actually, lots of neighbors seem to have gathered, so I squiggle around to see if maybe . . . but no. My heart, despite appearances, is running at about 8,000 rpm, so I can't be all that cool, although to be fair it's been at about 6,500 since I got the text.

"Wait!" the driver woman calls as I scoot off in the direction of the Blue house—it's brown—without even a little bit of further ado.

"Do it again," a guy yells from the sidewalk. "I didn't have my camera ready."

I get laughter and applause, and I wave over my head as I run, and realize my elbow is damn banged, but hey, what's an elbow but a broken arm with a hinge anyway, right?

The doorbell does not work at her house, but they never

bother fixing it or leaving a note or even putting a discouraging strip of tape across the thing, because the Blues would be just as happy if most people just went away, or better yet pressed the button a bunch of times and then went away, while the Blues watched from a window. So I knock, loud and fast and happy and nonstop until the door swings open.

Oh.

"Hey, Ronny." Ronny is June's fatherlike substance.

"Hey, O. Were you the dickwad slithering under traffic there on the corner?"

"How the hell did you see that?"

"I was at the upstairs window. None of your business."

Ronny and I don't get fantastically along.

"You going to let me in?"

"Why would I do that?"

Peeking around Ronny's shoulder is Leona, June's mom. I like Leona, more than a lot of people do. She's not bad, just mostly beat down by Ronny.

"Are you okay?" Leona asks me softly. "I heard Ronny at the window laughing something crazy, and he said you were squashed under a truck."

"I wasn't squashed, Leona, but thanks."

"Why are you here?" Ronny asks.

"I was summoned."

"Let the boy in, Ronny."

"Who summoned you?"

"Who do you think? June."

"June ain't here," he says.

"Let him in anyway. You want a drink or something, O?"

"She texted me. And told me to come here."

"Not here," Ronny says.

"Here," I say. "When somebody says 'come *over*,' if they don't say anywhere else, it means come over to the place where they live."

"That's true," Leona says, "but she really ain't here."

"Hiya, O," Maxine says, walking across my field of vision behind her parents. Maxie is June's older sister.

"Hiya, Maxie," I say.

"So ya see," Ronny says, "you weren't summoned here."

"Okay," I say. "So where is she?"

"She was here just a short while ago," Leona says. "She was here when I went to the drugstore, but then when I got back, she was gone already. Where is she, Ronny? D'ya know?"

"She went away. For a vacation."

This, is something. Ronny likes messing with me, always liked messing with me, even when he liked me, even though he never much liked me, but now when he clearly doesn't like me, he will mess with me beyond banter-type messing. And this, is something.

"Junie never takes a vacation. Never, ever."

"Well, that was before," Ronny says.

I hear a blender kick up and screamy-whine in the kitchen.

"Wouldja let the boy in, Ronny," Leona says, but it's not really a request, since she reaches from behind him and pulls me by the hand into the house.

"You want a smoothie?" Maxine says as I am seated at one of the high breakfast stools at the bar that separates the kitchen from the dining area.

"No, thank you," I say.

"How 'bout if I put a little rum in it?"

"Fine, I'll take the smoothie. But not the rum."

Ronny takes a seat at the kitchen side of the bar, diagonally across from me. Leona excuses herself and is gone in a sad puff of sigh. Maxine sits across from me and pounds two smoothie glasses down on the bar.

"That'll be ten cents, pardner," she says.

"Put it on my tab," I say. We clink glasses. "What do you mean, Ronny, 'that was before'? Before what? What was before?"

"Before she off-loaded you, of course. Ain't that obvious? I thought you was supposed to be smart. Maxie, wasn't this guy supposed to be smart?"

"He is smart, Dad. Shut up."

"Anyway, yeah, like I was saying, ah, the life Junie's leading these days, you wouldn't recognize it. She does stuff, you wouldn't believe it. Party stuff, guys . . . whoo the guys . . ."

I am boiling. I hate it when I'm boiling, because I have a face that announces to the whole world I am boiling. Fuchsia, I believe is the color.

"Look, he's boilin'," Ronny says, pointing and laughing like I'm in a glass display case.

"She does *nothin'*, O," Maxine says. "Don't listen to this guy. Nothin'. No guys, nothin'. She works the stupid store, she walks the dumb dogs. That's it."

The joy rising in my guts now, chasing the flush right out of my face, is something I should not be proud of. She should have a life. She deserves a life, and a fantastic one.

And she should be here.

"Where did she go, Ronny?" I ask with the slight crunch of demand in my voice that is never a good idea with this man.

"I told you," he snarls, "vacation."

I turn to Maxine, my palms upturned to catch some help.

"No idea, O. I just got home. Why don't you just call her?"

Ronny laughs and points a bread stick at me, and I realize the extra awfulness of making his day like I am.

"Because I'm a dope," I say, pulling out my phone and pressing her number.

In a couple of seconds the room tinkles with small music. Small music and big laughter.

The music sounds just like one of those little kids' plinky toy pianos, playing "Hello, Dolly!" Junie's ring tone. The laughter is Ronny.

"June's phone," I say, looking all around, at the counter and the floor and the Blues across the bar from me, because that's where the sound is coming from.

Maxine turns sideways in her chair, scowls, and reaches down into the vicinity of Ronny's back pocket. When she produces the phone and he produces a higher volume of laughter, she biffs him right on the side of the head with the phone.

"Was it you? Texting me?" I ask him.

That sucks the mirth right out of him. "Hell, no," he snaps. "I don't think so."

"Where *is* she?" I shout. I don't care how angry or violent he gets now, because this is not the way it should be going. "Junie never ever goes anywhere without her phone. She doesn't go to the bathroom without her phone. She doesn't even shower without it."

"And you would know these things how?"

"Come *on*, Ronny. I'm really getting worried here."

"Don't get worried. You got nothing to worry about. You know why? 'Cause you got no business with my daughter anymore."

"Christ, just tell him where she is, Dad."

Maxine seems utterly unconcerned, which should relax me some but relaxes me none.

"She is on vacation, just like I said."

"Where on vacation? Who with?"

"Listen," Ronny says, standing up. The way a guy stands up. You need to take notice when a guy stands up that way, especially a guy like Ronny. "I have to politely point out that you are out of line. That, lest you forget, my daughter dumped you and she has a life of her own and it is none of your damn business where she goes or who she goes with. I have to politely point out that you are entitled to none of the information you are demanding, but I will tell you she left here a short while ago in the company of a man, and I point this out only because it pleases me to do so. And now I will politely point you in the direction of the exit."

"Polite my ass," Maxine says, shoving her father back down onto his seat and walking around to my side of the bar. She takes me by the arm as we walk to the door.

"Sorry about that, O," she says. "You know how he is. If I get anything more out of him, I'll let you know."

"Thanks, Maxie," I say.

When we get to the door, Leona appears, standing in the doorway that leads to the living room. She looks haunted, fragile.

"Where is she, Ma?" Maxine says flatly. "I bet you do

know. Wouldja just say, so he can not worry a little bit?"

It would not be correct to call the noise from the kitchen a bark. If a bear put its voice into a bark, it would sound like this.

"LeOna!" Ronny calls.

Leona raises her hand to cover her mouth and nose. Her sigh hisses through the grille of her fingers before she turns and walks back into the living room.

"What is wrong with you?" Mom says when I've made my third lap of the house. I pace. When I'm trying to think or to unthink, I pace, which makes the machinery of my mind far too visible to the people who know me well.

"Nothing," I say, passing her right by.

She is sitting at the dining room table, sketching. She has her own study, where most of her contracted commercial design crap gets done, but when she's in itch-a-sketch mode looking for inspiration, she plunks down wherever the plunkin's good.

"Your sweat stains say otherwise," she says.

It takes about twenty seconds at this pace for me to make the circuit—living room, hallway, dining room, kitchen, hallway, living room again—which gives us both good time to compose snappy retorts for each other by the time I pass through her space once more.

"Sweat doesn't speak," I say.

"Neither do you, and that's not healthy. What's wrong?"

"Are you sketching me?"

"Of course I am."

"Cut it out. You know I hate it."

"I'll stop if you stop."

She has a giant portfolio of her me-as-salesman portraits. I look like my father, I suppose, only less successful.

"Want to see?" she says as I sit across the table from her.

I nod weakly.

Okay, this one is different. She has drawn me the way cartoonists draw two characters chasing each other around a tree—just a blur of circular lines with what looks like my nose and furrowed brow emerging somewhere in the middle of it.

"That's instantly my favorite," I say.

She looks far more pleased than this kind of statement should make a person. I have to remember how much she cares what I think, what I say. I have not always used my powers wisely there.

"I'm going to frame it," she says, signing the corner carefully. "You going to talk?"

I think about it. I decide I am. Sort of.

"There's nothing to say," I say. "I'm just a little concerned about Junie. But it's probably nothing."

She turns the page in her big sketchbook and starts with

the telltale scratchy-sounding strokes and furtive glances that mean I'm sketch material again.

"Jesus, Mom . . ."

"Shush. Stay still. I mean, don't shush. But do stay still."

"Fine. Well, we're not together anymore, so it's really none of my business. . . ."

"You are going to have to move on somehow, unfortunately. It's going to take some time, and some pain."

"I know. But it's not just that . . ."

"Speaking of Junie, did you hear that that awful man over there, that One Who Knows character, won the lottery? Again?"

"What?"

"Yes. Rumor has it that he's *won* the lottery. *Again*." My mother hates the way people do air quotation marks with their fingers, and she is constantly at war with what she considers to be the corroding effects of all things cliché, so at times like this, when she says words like those—"won" and "again"—to register her scorn she puts them in italics by placing her hands karate chop fashion alongside her face at 45 degree angles and chopping the air. That she also goes bug-eyed and lurches forward when she does it is, I believe, involuntary.

"Where did you hear that *rumor*?" I say, chopping crazed italics in the air.

"Your father brought it home from the office, naturally."

If there is a financial transaction, legitimate or otherwise, that happens in this state at ten in the morning, those guys are discussing it over lunch.

He's not a bad guy, my father. But if water were money, he'd be a fish.

And as for money folk, they don't come any fishier than One Who Knows. He may not have actually won the lottery that time a few years back, but he certainly collected it. Very publicly too, so everyone could see. See, it is commonly known in that neighborhood that anyone in the area who wins the lottery in any meaningful way should come to Juan with the ticket. I was never clear about what the deal on offer was, but I got the impression it involved the winner being paid a generous chunk of the cover price of that windfall, tax free, combined with a job for life and all the fringe benefits implied by joining the select company of Juan's nearest and dearest.

And if the famously work-shy Juan was able to show everybody, especially his ninety-seven-year-old mom and his neighbors and the Internal Revenue Service his great honest good fortune on the evening news, well, a feel-good story all over it surely was.

A sweet deal, some might say, and one reason the man so famously splashes out on tickets for almost everybody he meets. If you couldn't really tell which tickets you bought on your own and which were the result of the large largesse of the man himself, well, then maybe all tickets were his tickets. He spikes the punch, it's his buzz as much as yours.

He tended to see it that way anyway.

"Good for him," I say. "Such a lucky, lucky guy, huh?"

"Indeed. Hey, maybe he would like to have his portrait done to commemorate the fortuitous moment. I could do that thing they do, the Roman emperor approach, where I do him from the shoulders up, robe hanging off him, hair all slicked down and ringed with a laurel wreath?"

I picture it and I laugh, and some of the tension I felt earlier washes away as I watch the crinkly lines at the corners of my mother's eyes deepen. She is happy, grinning away and scribbling, and this is something we can enjoy, do enjoy, having fun at somebody's minor expense. But somebody who invites it, of course.

"Hey," I suddenly say. "You're doing it to *me* right now, aren't you?"

She giggles and scribbles.

"Fine," I sigh. "Show me."

Yup indeed. It's toga-party me, laurel leaves and all, and she has even gone to the trouble of giving me those Roman bangs that make it look like I cut my own hair. And I *still* look like I'm selling something.

"Can I have it?" I ask.

She is beaming, like a kid.

"It's not that big a deal, Mom. I wish you wouldn't be like this. It puts a lot of pressure on me."

She is signing the portrait with a flourish. "And God knows you don't need any more of that, Mr. Pace Car. You're pretty torqued up already."

"Yeah. It's just . . . Yeah, sorry. I'll be all right."

She hands me over the sketch and then goes all weird coy on me.

"Listen, if you need to . . ." She does this awkward head tilt and thumb point in the direction of upstairs, and the pained expression that comes over her makes me sympathy wince.

"What?" I say. "If I need to what?"

"You knowwww." She drags it out agonizingly. "You might have to . . . *relax*, and I'll just leave you to it. I won't bother—"

"Mom!" I say, and jump up from the table. I instinctively know that I will someday laugh my head off at this, but right now I am far, far too mortified, and so is she.

"I'm sorry," she says, biting her knuckle. "I was just trying to relieve . . . You look so . . ."

"I'm fine, Mom," I say, launching into what looks like my pacing pattern but is in fact a roundabout dash for the door.

"Yes," she says. "That's better anyway. A good brisk walk, that will sort you out."

Sort me out. By the time I pull the front door closed behind me, I am already almost to the point where I can laugh. But that's probably more from the relief of escape than anything else.

My mother *always* has my best interest at heart, but we both really need to get out of the house more.

I am standing at the Blues' door again, with the rolled-up portrait of Caligula O'Brien in my hands.

"I thought I threw you out on your ear," Ronny says, both smiling and snarling. He likes to be displeased.

It's one of the reasons he and I are such a great match.

"I brought a present for my girlfriend," I say.

"O," I hear Maxie call from off in the distance. "What are you *do*in'? I told you I'd let you know. You *tryin'* to get the man to punch you in the head?"

"One," Ronny says, holding up his thumb, "she ain't here. Like I already told you. Two," he says, adding the pinky finger for styling purposes, "she ain't your girlfriend. And three"—he adds the ring finger, and now I am certain he practices this—"are you *tryin'* to get me to punch you in the head?"

The rain has stopped, but the air is still so heavy with warm damp that it hardly matters, and it doesn't seem like I'll be invited inside anytime soon. I kick anxiously at the concrete two-step of the Blues' stoop, and I persevere.

"I'm not trying to get you to do anything of the kind, Ronny, I assure you, but something's wrong here, I can feel it, and if I have to take a punch in the head to find out what's going on with Junie, then I am prepared to—"

Bam.

Right in the side of the head. Ronny's unfeasibly big fist with its twelve or thirteen gnarled and calloused knuckles crashes down on me, and I crash right down, on the step, on the sidewalk, on my ass. I feel splits in the structure of my skull, almost making that crackly splintering noise a tree makes when it falls.

But it's only pain.

He stands over me, fists on his hips, lips pursed, growling. Despite what has happened he is somehow the one furious.

"You think you can come here and tell *me* there is something wrong in my own household, and that *you* are here to straighten it out?"

The left side of my head is a busy little airport of pain planes coming and going, fast and noisy and relentless. If it were balanced, even—if both sides of me felt the same—that would be better, but this is making me want to flop sideways and smother it all out.

"Yeah," I say, perhaps out of sarcasm, or perhaps in an attempt to get him to put me out of my misery, "that's what I think."

He comes down the two slick concrete steps to the slick sidewalk, where I manage to kind of balance awkwardly on one hip and an elbow. He crouches, in his shiny gray shorts, crouches like a catcher, and what I catch is the scent of Satan in his crotch, a sulfuric ammonia eau de cologne that makes me say "Oh" and cover my nose the way I should probably be covering up my face against the beating coming my way.

"Do you know who I am?" he hisses.

I nod, keeping it simple in case it's a trick question.

"Do you know who I work for?"

Now I see where he's going, and he doesn't *work* for the guy. He toadies. He's a toad, even among toads, as his own daughter told me on many a shame-filled evening.

"Yes," I say.

"Well, little rich boy, who, then? Who do I work for?"

I am not rich. Athletes and senators and guys with their own TV churches are rich. Granted, I don't notice how much a shirt costs until the cashier asks for my card, so I'm not exactly hurting. But rich is a whole other category, I think.

"The One," I say, and maybe it's a mild concussion or the chloroform coming at me from between Ronny's legs, but fear and pain and weakness are fading—I'm sure temporarily.

"The One Who Knows. That's goddamn right, boy."

"This is good," I say. "I always wanted to ask somebody, an insider like yourself. What, exactly, is it, that he knows?"

"Ha-*hah!*" Maxine laughs from somewhere not too far off.

"Shut it, Maxine," Ronny says as he grabs me hard by the

collar in just that way that truly hard, mean, and dangerous people grab.

I will mock, and have mocked, Ronny's intelligence. His hygiene, his style, his overall meaninglessness. But no one will ever hear me mock his toughness. He is the real kind of hard, brutal, vicious, and right now I could well do something that will make me smell as bad as him.

"Leave him alone," Maxie says, and I realize she is in the doorway. I love Maxine.

"Go in the house," he says, and while he is as serious and poisonous as ever, I am a little thrilled to hear a small something else in there, something that acknowledges Maxine's *something*. The fact that she is not afraid of him? The fact that there is something of the vicious in her as well?

Whatever it is, I love-love it, and her.

"I'll go in the house when you come with me," she says.

He pauses, hangs on to my shirt. He inhales deeply, exhales with purpose, hot and hideous down into my face, and it's like he can switch to extra noxious when he needs to, and it is as foul as hell indeed.

Finally he shoves me down, down-er, onto my back. "Watch yourself," he says, and then snatches the sketch, the portrait my mother did, my gift for Junie to see whenever she does come home so she can see me again and she can laugh at me properly again and we can get right again, for good again.

"Hey, hey, don't scrunch that," I say as I see him scrunching it in his big ignorant paw.

He unsurprisingly ignores the command until he gets to the doorway and Maxie snaps "Don't scrunch it" as he passes.

She comes down quickly, gives me a hand up, checks me out.

"You okay?" she says, whispery-tough-sweet. She didn't see the punch, so probably figures he just shoved me playfully down the stairs or something.

"Yeah," I say, checking myself to see how true that actually is. My balance feels good. Less than perfect. But good.

"Okay. So you can get yourself home all right?"

"Yeah," I say.

"Good," she snaps. "Then go there and *stay* there this time." She gives me a seeing-me-on-my-way slap to the back of the head that on most occasions would be almost fun but right now causes tears to spill down my face as I walk, weak and wobbly, away.

"I'll call you," she calls. I raise a hand of acknowledgment as I stagger on.

I am halfway home when my phone goes off. I stop, because to see the screen I must focus.

It's Junie's number.

"Hey," I say, all excited, all stupid. "Hey-hey."

"Come back here," commands the awful growly-bear voice. Then he hangs up.

I stand in the middle of the sidewalk staring at the screen of my phone, like it's going to give me advice or something. Maybe he's going to punch the other side of my head, to balance me out. Maybe he's going to tell me, finally, where June is. There is no figuring, but there is also no choice. I have to go back.

Somehow it seems my equilibrium is slightly worse on the trip back, but my pace still quickens.

No need to knock. He's been watching for me.

"Get in," Ronny says.

I follow as he leads me back once more to the breakfast bar. There he has spread out the portrait of me as the emperor. It feels really embarrassing now, with Ronny here. And he did scrunch it, the chin now looking like it has a wiry goatee.

"Why is that out?" I ask.

"Because it's damn cute," Maxine says.

"Please," I say. "Please, don't . . ."

"No, no," Ronny says, tapping the portrait with his middle finger and looking like he is giving it serious contemplation. "It's very good. It makes you look . . . like a real somebody. Who did this?"

"My mother."

"Really?" he says, very impressed. He looks up from the sketch to stare at me, working out whether I am leveling with him or not. I'm pretty sure he thought all portraits were done in a booth machine at CVS or the carnival. "Really? Your mother?"

"Yeah, really. Is there any aspirin or something?"

Maxine pats my shoulder on her way past to get me something. Now my shoulder hurts.

"This is beautiful work. Your mother is very talented. Tell her I said so, and I want one."

Maxine reenters the room, drops two tablets into my hand, and grabs me a glass with the remnants of somebody's smoothie. Thank God we can assume it wasn't Ronny's.

"What are these?" I garble after the tablets are already in my mouth.

"Aspirin's friends," she says, motioning for me to get the smoothie down me. I comply.

"Thanks," I say to her. Then "Thanks," I say to the hulking source of the pain in the first place. "My mother is proud of her work. She'll be pleased to hear the praise."

"And the commission," he reminds me.

"Right," I say. "I'll check with her, see if she's got the time. . . . She's really busy with—"

As I am talking, Ronny returns to studying the portrait but at the same time mimes a *Call your mother* gesture using his thumb and pinkie held to the side of his head like a phone.

He could go whole days talking with his fingers, I think.

I pretend to call my mother, pretend to get her answering machine, pretend to leave an enthusiastic message about this wonderful commission she will be doing over my dead body or pieces thereof.

My head is swimming, in a lot of senses. I want to have as little to do with Ronny Blue as possible, and I want my mother to have even less to do with him. Having any kind of business arrangement with him is a truly horrifying proposition. And yet, Mom will want to do it, I know. She is fearless and ambitious and loves portraiture regardless of the unseemliness of the character, and in fact she is collecting something of a rogues gallery of faces for some ultimate artistic purpose, and for that, Ronny Blue makes an obvious poster boy.

And I need to stay connected. To these people. To June.

And the other swim my head is doing is more of a treading water.

I am floating. There is no pain. There is no worry. There is the equilibrium issue still . . . but so what? Doesn't seem to matter.

"I'm gonna take you home," Maxie says, putting one hand on my back and the other gently under my elbow the way you do when you help an elderly person across the street.

"Really?" I say. "That's nice of you."

"Yeah," she says, "well, I'm a nice kinda girl."

• • •

"You know what I would like?" Maxie says, her hand around my waist as we make our way up the road. The sun is just starting to work an orange cigarette burn through the gray fabric of the clouds.

I reflexively look down at her hand on my hip, then turn to her close-by face. I can just about feel the stupid of my smile as I say, "*You* know what *I* would like?"

"Yeah, I do. Well, you're not getting that, so shut up."

"Where'd you get those friends of the aspirin?"

"I got them from the friend of the pharmacist. Shush. What I want is for you to talk to your mom about doing a portrait."

"Please, Maxie, don't make my mom draw that awful man in a toga."

"Not that fathead. My mother. Do you think you could talk to your ma about doing my ma? I think it would be friggin' beautiful, I really do. And she deserves it."

"She deserves something, that's for sure. Hey, Maxie?"

"Yeah?"

"What about Junie?"

"What about her?"

"She's gone, that's what? She's vanished, and nobody seems to be bothered about this but me."

"First, she ain't vanished. She's just, someplace, I don't

know. Second, she's tougher than Turkish Taffy, that kid. Nobody worries about Junie."

"I worry about her."

"That's because you're a big ol' nancy boy and you're in love with her."

"I'm not . . . Never said I was in love with her."

"Good," she says, turning me manually around the corner to my street. "'Cause you're dumped, remember?"

"Ah, she didn't mean that. She was lying. Sweet Junie Blue Lies and Lyin' O'Brien. That's who we are. That's what we do."

Maxie stops as we reach the sidewalk in front of my house. She looks the place down and up, down to its rampant rosebushes creeping their way up the trellises, up to its yellow brick colonial square face with all the windows and the handsome surging gables. She is shaking her head in a kind of wonderment.

"She wasn't lyin', O'Brien. I'm sorry about that, but she meant it. However, if it makes you feel any better, I think she's crazy."

"You do?" I say, and feel a very stupid heart-flutter over this.

"Absolutely. I'd do you for the house alone."

Flutter subsides. "It's not that nice a house," I say.

"Sure it is. It's a nice house, you're a nice guy, your mom

is a nice artist, and your dad, whoever he is and whatever he does, is a superior piece of work to my shit-ass father. Can I take a rose home to my ma?"

My mother is crazy-protective of her garden, and especially her roses. She has yellow and bloodred and pink, and they look like she makes them up individually in her studio. I couldn't possibly—

"Wait. Don't pick," Mom says from behind the first-floor window screen. "I'll go get my pruning shears."

"Mom!" I snap at her nosy little vapor trail.

"I think I should draw her with the roses all around her, in her hair, in the background," Mom says, lost in her excited creative cloud as she arranges flowers at the kitchen sink.

"That would be friggin' lovely," Maxine says, sipping her Earl Grey tea.

"Friggin' lovely," Mom echoes, giggling. "How about I throw in some friggin' baby's breath as well?"

"Is she makin' fun of me?" Maxine whispers, and in her flashing eye I see a small bolt of what makes her father scary.

"Absolutely, positively not," I say, and as soon as I say it, I see the total opposite thing, the bright and open unguarded joy that makes her sister such nip to a cat like me.

"Breathe on it, baby," Maxine says cheerily.

My mom is about as happy as she gets, doing this, and

Maxine is clearly getting a lot for her money today, scoring a professional-quality bouquet for her mother as well as scheduling a sitting for her mother's surely once-in-a-lifetime portrait.

This is pure contentment, then, right?

Right?

"He's been mooning around the house ever since she dumped him," Mom offers even though nobody anywhere asked.

"Okay, Mom. Thanks. Flowers ready to go yet?"

"It is sad," Maxie says, kind of neutral. "Maybe it'll work out. He's a good boy."

"He is," Mom says almost urgently. "He's a very good boy."

"And I'm not just for Christmas," I say, as long as they seem to think I'm a dog. Though if I were a dog, maybe Junie would be here right now, walking me.

"I was just telling him outside that I think Junie was crazy, dumping him."

Jeez, Maxine, stop there. Don't say the thing about the house.

"I love your house, by the way," she says, slipping me a deadly smile.

"Thank you," Mom says. "It feels a bit vacant some days, and with this one maybe leaving soon. Might be time to downsize."

"I'll move in," Maxie says.

"Aren't you sweet," Mom says, handing the flowers over as if Maxine just won Miss Universe. Which I believe she could—as long as Junie weren't a contestant. Which she'd never be because of how she feels about it. One of her stated goals in life is to vomit on a reigning Miss Universe.

"Well, then," Mom says as we see Maxie to the door. "You check with your mother about the dates, and we'll get things going. I'll want her to come for a few sittings, as it's much more serious than when I dash off those silly trifles of my son."

"Oh, my father wants one of those trifles of himself, as a matter of fact."

"Well," Mom says, sincerely breathless now. "I guess your family is going to keep me well occupied in the near future. This is going to be sweet."

Occupied, oh yes. Sweet? Maybe sweet-and-sour.

Maxine bounces down the steps and across the lawn—which Mom graciously overlooks—clutching her flowers and whistling.

"She whistles," Mom says, taking both my hands in hers after the door closes. "Isn't that marvelous? Hardly anybody whistles anymore."

Three

I'm walking on the beach with my father.
It's Sunday. We do this frequently on Sundays. We don't
have a whole lot of interaction on the other six days because
he works lunatic hours (at the job he describes as "cloning
money in my lab—theoretically"), but doing that seems to
make him really happy, which makes him a pretty pleasant
guy, which makes our Sundays something to look forward to.
I don't need tax or investment advice or life insurance, and
so I don't have anything tangible he could be after, so I can
only conclude that the warmth and humor he shows me on
the beach on Sundays has something to do with me and him
and us, which fills me with something nice. I wonder how
different it is for people who do have something he wants.

We don't go to church like Mom does. We are each other's
Sunday service.

Sunday is sacred.

"So, your mother tells me you're really at it lately," he
says, staring down a seagull that is after his fried clam necks.

"At what?"

"You know, the ol' sock puppet. Up in your room."

"Jesus, Dad, what is it with you two? I am fine. I am normal."

"Calm down, Son. Nobody said it wasn't normal. Hell, when I was your age, I left a snail trail of Vaseline from—"

"Dad, stop!"

He's shaking his head and laughing, either at my discomfort or at the memory of his demented adolescent self.

"Wait," he gasps. "You haven't even heard the part about when the frenzies got so bad once I accidentally grabbed the Vicks VapoRub instead of—"

I snatch the little bucket of clams out of his hand and sling the whole thing up toward the seagull, who dives onto the contents and is joined within seconds by all his shrieking pals.

My father stares forlornly as they devour his Sunday snack. It's the only day he allows himself fried food.

"Your mother's right," he says. "You are extremely tense."

All you can do in these situations is sigh. So I sigh at him.

"You were right, though," he continues. "If a guy is going to eat deep fried one day a week, then the damn clams should at least have bellies. That was an embarrassment, and I'm frankly surprised the seagulls don't just send them back. The seagulls around here have no self-respect."

The low-self-esteem seagulls have made short work of the embarrassing clams and are now pursuing us up the beach for more, screaming and diving at us. Suddenly I feel, and hear, the telltale *plap* of getting dumped on.

Dad, unscathed as usual, looks at my newly decorated shoulder and puts a bit more space between us.

"I guess they are sending them back, in a way, huh?"

"Good one, Dad," I say. Then my eyes can no longer resist the glow of the shiny white excrescence that is beaconing like the military shoulder bling of a dictator-general. "Jeez," I say, looking at it, "what, did they all collaborate on this thing?"

"Either that or a Pegasus just flew over. C'mon, kid, I'll buy you a new T-shirt. And some proper clams."

Ten minutes later my dad and I are sitting across from each other at a picnic table on the boulevard overlooking the beach. It's still early-ish season, and it's breezy and overcast, so the space is largely quiet, largely ours, largely perfect. I have on my new foolish orange tie-dye T-shirt with a surf-board on the front. In the trash can by the souvenir kiosk is my soiled, lost, and unlamented previous shirt. That one had no embarrassing kitsch on it but did have some prominent designer branding, which made it actually easier for me to part with. I hate wearing advertisements for the manufac-turers, but because I am a lazy and passive consumer and my mother bought me that shirt and because it was a particularly fetching forest green, I wore it a lot. I'm glad it's gone.

"We'll get you another one of those," Dad says.

"Sure," I say, because I am meaningless. "But if I really wanted to, I could probably wash that one fine."

"There will be no Pegasus shit in our household," he says. But I already knew that. "Persnickety" would describe my dad, to the point where, not only would I never expect to drag home Pegasus droppings, but on the rare occasion (twice ever, to my knowledge) when he ever steps in more common droppings, he has to buy new running shoes before even coming home. He had to run an extra seven miles one time.

The clams, on the other hand, are magnificent. As is everything else. We both got the same thing, the large fisherman's platter, which has fried clams and scallops and haddock and massive butterfly shrimp and thick crispy-out/fluffy-in french fries that taste miraculously of seafood. Ketchup and tartar sauce are both along for the ride and almost make up for the crime of one ice cream scoop of coleslaw that threatened to infect everything before we banished it. Root beers with actual creamy heads bring the whole thing home.

Dad is chewing and staring at his plate, gesturing at it with two priest-blessing hands. "I love this more than my own offspring."

"Nice, Dad. Thanks."

"What? You think I'm your *father*? Your mother was supposed to tell you . . ."

This is our Sunday service. I would stack it against anybody's.

My phone beeps a message. I am still sweating the Junie situation enough that I jump every time. Normally I would let it beep and defer to Dad and fried seafood.

"Must be serious," Dad says as I read.

Call me please now. I love you.

"I have to call, Dad. I'm really sorry. I'll just be a second."

"Fine," he says. "You gotta do what you gotta do."

Normally this is the type of thing that would irritate him—on Sunday. But he is being very understanding as I step away from the table and walk toward the sea.

Then I look quickly back over my shoulder and catch him kidnapping a butterfly shrimp. He fills the vacancy in my plate with fries.

"Nice, Dad," I say again. He looks pleased to have been caught.

Come on, Junie, answer.

"Hello?" I say when there is a silent answer. "Hello? Junie? Come on. What is it?"

"Oh, Aunty Em, Aunty Em, I'm frightened—"

I stare off into the distance, into the wind and the surf as the man works the humiliation deep into the wound.

"You're an unbelievably awful guy, Ronny," I say as calmly as I can into his cackling laughter. "Where is she? Is she back yet?"

"What about my portrait? When should I come over?"

A shudder, a real, honest-to-hell full-body ripple runs all

up and down me at the thought of this man in my home.

"I'm working on it," I say, probably unconvincingly.

"You promised me."

"In actuality I never quite—"

"Don't you dare go thinking that your mother's gonna do Leona before me. I don't know who you think you're playin' here, kid, but that ain't happenin'. I don't play."

"I never believed that you did. Play. I was—"

"Screwin' with me, yeah. You was just screwin' with me is what you was doin'. Don't get cute with me, boy, or it'll be your sorriest day ever. You and Maxine go thinkin' you're gonna make a dope out of Ronny Blue, you got somethin' else comin'."

I think of the angles on that. Of how it could be possible for anyone to make any more of a dope of Ronny Blue. About how half the reason I am getting this earful is that he's not man enough to try it with Maxie, and I think again how much I would like to be her when I grow up. I think of those angles and some other clever ones, and then I step up and take the more me angle.

"Nobody's making a dope of you, Ronny."

"Good. 'Cause if anybody tried to cut in line and get my wife's picture done before *mine*—if I even let her get one at all—then it might be a little bit of a shame 'cause of how she's gonna look come picture day, and who wants a picture of that, huh?"

"Hey," my dad calls, done with being patient on a Sunday.

"Who would want that, huh?" I say to the awfulest guy there is.

"Right. So fix this up. And do be in touch."

"I—"

He apparently has no need to hear my continuing thoughts on the subject.

"What was that?" Dad says, looking at me with one eye squinted, the way he always looks when somebody tries to sell *him* something.

"Nothin'," I say.

Now both eyes are squinted. "Dropping our *g*'s all of a sudden?"

"Noth*ing*, Father. Anyway, what is *this*?" I gesture at my fisherman's platter, which has clearly been tampered with.

"Seagulls," he says. "I wish you'd been here. You would have been so proud of me. I fought them off heroically, at great risk to myself. I shouted at them as I flailed away. I said, This succulent fisherman's platter belongs to my special boy, you big screeching feathered bastards, especially the clams, and to a lesser extent the butterfly shrimp, and if you think you are getting away with them, well, you can just take me, too! It was quite epic. Are you sure you didn't hear it? You were right over there. . . . Oh, that's right. You were on your phone. On a Sunday."

You have to respect the rituals of the true believer.

"Sorry, Dad. You're right. Thing is, that was Ronny Blue."

"*Ronny* Blue."

"Ronny Blue."

"Not Junie Blue."

"Ronny Blue."

"Rotten Ronny?"

"That's the one.

"Scumbag Ronny Blue?"

"I think we have identified which Ronny Blue it was, Dad."

"What's he want with you?"

I finish the last of the scallops and clams. Dad has been out of seafood for a while now and is social-picking at the fries. The gulls are gathering like a sinister gang around us.

"Actually, Dad, it's what he wants with your wife, more than me."

The fry falls right out of his hand and lands under the table, provoking a frightening seagull scrum right there between his feet. In his shorts, with those legs, he could be in jeopardy if there is a nearsighted bird in the crowd, but he is oblivious to them.

"What?"

"Yeah, Dad. It's Mom he's rooting around for."

His face fills with a rush of blood, which then flushes right back out again like in a human head cistern.

"Son, you are absolutely decimating Sunday right now."

I stand up and surrender the beachhead—the tabletop—to the seagulls and wave Dad to walk with me. "He wants her to do a portrait of him. That's all," I say, laughing as much as I honestly can when Ronny Blue is even part of the subject.

"Oh, thank God," he says, a hand flat on his thrumping heart. My father has a lot of great qualities, and I know I can count on him for almost anything. But if it came down to an interfamily rumble, I think I'd take Mom with me.

"So, you're cool with Ronald McDouchebag coming by and putting his feet under your table sometime this week?"

He keeps walking, keeps that hand glued to that chest.

"See, I was just calming down there. Really, you are simply slaughtering this Sunday for me."

"Ah, Dad," I say, putting an arm across his shoulders and pulling him hard into me. "It won't be a huge deal. We'll figure out something to get the thing done and over with. I'll tell you what I'm really upset about, though, if you're up for it."

"Oh, absolutely, that would be wonderful. Anything to get my mind off that terrible thing you just told me. Shoot."

I laugh, shove him away from me. "I'm really glad we can spend this kind of quality time together, Dad, and to know you're there for me."

"Great. Now hurry up and tell me your awful thing so I can forget my awful thing."

"Ha. Well, our awful things are related, as it happens."

"Okay, tell," he says seriously. "I'm listening."

On the way back to the car, I unburden myself to my father. I tell him how much the whole situation with Junie Blue has been killing me anyway, and how now the thing with the weirdness of her "vacation" is just overwhelming my thoughts completely. Telling him does make me feel a little bit better, even though it will have no practical application.

"She is a wonderful girl," he says, looking at me across the new-penny copper roof of his low-slung Mitsubishi. "It's going to be a lot of work to ever do as well as her again."

"Thanks, Dad."

"I didn't say you weren't capable, just that it will be hard work. Speaking of work . . ."

He has this vision of me and him in the family business together, shoulder to shoulder spending our days convincing people that really, their money and our money is really all the same thing. I have no such vision, but no competing vision to counter him with, and therefore no stomach for the vision/career/future discussion in any of its forms.

"Dad, unlock the car. I'm begging you."

"But . . . you have such a great vocabulary," he says desperately.

I laugh out loud at him. "Well, whoop-de-shit to that, Dad."

"See, there it is."

"What's a vocabulary got to do with anything, Dad?"

Here's one of the many things that make my dad singular. As well as I know him, I never know. Never know what serious thing is going to make him laugh. Never know what neutral nothing is going to pull him up all grim and serious.

"*Everything*. It's got everything to do with everything. How you talk. How you carry yourself. How you present and how you relate. Those are the keys to absolutely everything, and you have got all that. You think I'm a success because I am some kind of financial wizard? Pffft. I don't know bo diddly about finance. I know how to relate, Son, and that is what counts."

"That's ev—"

"And golf," he adds. "All that, and golf. That's what counts."

"If you unlock the car," I say with folded prayer hands before my face, "I promise to give this a lot of thought."

"Promise?"

My hands remain folded, my manner solemn. "Not really."

His manner goes perky. "I'm going to take that as a 'We'll see.'"

We get in, and in seconds he is zipping his way up the boulevard and I have my window wide open, my head hanging out there doglike in the direction of the surf, the scent, the sacred stuff.

"You think Ronny Rat has done something bad to her?"

Dad ventures when he feels enough time and wind have blown through my head.

I pause. "I don't know," I say.

He pauses. "You want me to go over and kick his ass?" he says.

We both pause. But just.

"Bwa-hah-hah-hah . . . ," we burst out together.

Another vital sacred part of Sunday used to be the walk over to Junie's neighborhood, to the corner shop, to buy a newspaper from her. It would be late in the day, and I would pass about five thousand copies of the same papers piled up in other shops along the way, much of the news already old, so it wasn't the most practical of trips. But I always looked forward to it, always brought her something from my mother's kitchen, since baking and soup-making were another part of the Sunday sacreds of our home life, even though Junie worked in a shop all day and could snack as much as she wanted to.

But those snacks wouldn't be my mother's cran-blueberry muffins, that's for sure, and they wouldn't be her coconut crab soup, that's for sure. And if, what-ho-lookit-the-time, I just happened to show up within an hour of closing time, then hanging around and being a pest followed by walking the lady home was just one more element making a sacred Sunday sacred, was it not?

Until she told me to cut it out. Until she told me I had to leave her and her Sundays the hell alone finally.

That left a bit of a hole, that did.

"Come on. Come out and play some tennis. Stop the moping."

It's my friend Malcolm, who has appeared quite mysteriously somewhere down there beneath my bedroom window. I am lying on my bed, not bothering the universe in any way and so reasonably expecting the universe to reciprocate. Malcolm has not interrupted a Sunday of mine since I stopped playing soccer and tennis after Junior year.

"I'm not moping. I'm relaxing."

"You'll get hairy hands," he says, really loudly. It has always been a defining characteristic of Malcolm's that he seems to believe there is a dedicated line of communication between himself and whomever he is communicating with, and the world at large cannot hear.

"Thanks anyway, Malcolm."

"Come on," he yells. "I have two rackets here and a full can of balls. Which is more than you can say."

I go to my window, kneel down, and press my forehead against the screen. "It's Sunday, for God's sake."

"So? Is your religion anti-tennis?"

"Why are you here?"

"Tennis," he says, holding up the equipment to prove it. "Like I told you."

And Malcolm is a man of truth. He says precisely what he means, usually at great volume, and often even when you wish he would be less straightforward.

"Right," I say, "but why now? I haven't seen you in ages."

"That's because I didn't know you got dumped. Sorry about that, by the way."

"Thanks. Who told you?"

"Your dad."

Grrr.

"Thanks, Dad!" I call out.

"Your mother put me up to it," he calls back. From the garage. Waxing his car is a sacred.

"Thanks, Mom!" I call out.

"You don't have to yell," Malcolm says, pointing at the floor below with a racket held like a machine gun. "She's right there at the window."

I hear a *Shush* so loud, it makes the rosebushes in the garden rustle.

"Fine," I say. "If everybody wants me to play tennis, I'll play tennis."

I am just pushing away from my window when I see Malcolm nod repeatedly and grin toward that downstairs window, and my mother loud-whispers, "Yes!"

Have I gotten this pathetic?

"In a word, yes," Malcolm says as we head down the street

toward the public courts. We could play at Dad's club, but the local courts are closer, quieter, and not infested with little rocket-propelled-snots who've been taking lessons since they were two and stare up at their own radar-gun readings for twenty seconds every time they serve an ace. Yes, radar guns.

"It was a rhetorical question, Malcolm. The kind that not only does not demand an answer but, if you are a good friend, doesn't even suggest one."

"Or, to look at it another way, if you're a really, really good friend, and honest, you are duty-bound to provide one."

"Okay, so if you are that level of friend, how did you let me *get* this pathetic?"

"Easy. You dumped me."

"What? I never dumped you. Anyway, that doesn't even make sense. Guys don't dump each other. They just . . . are, or not."

"No, you dumped me, Hamlet. You dumped all sub-Junie life-forms once you guys connected. And now that you are dumped, with me being me and nature abhorring a vacuum, I am attempting to fill the probably unfillable space that was occupied by the exquisite Junie Blue. By the way, for the record, you did very well for yourself there, while it lasted. Even though I still don't appreciate being dumped."

"You were not—"

"If a guy has to be dumped for somebody, it's almost an

honor to be dumped for the likes of the lovely Ms. Blue."

It's kind of a nice thing for him to say. It kind of hurts to be reminded.

"Well, thanks. I guess."

"Can I ask her out?"

"Sure," I say brightly. "Can I kill you?"

"Oh, I see. A skill you picked up hanging around the Blue household?"

"What, Ronny? He's no killer."

"No, he's not. He's also not such a bad guy, actually."

"He's not . . . Compared to what? And where did you come up with that?"

We have arrived at the courts, and as I figured, they are all ours. They are only a couple of blocks from the beach, and are cracked asphalt. But I feel like I know every crack, and so it's almost a plus.

"I played tennis with him once," Malcolm says as he slips his racket out of its case and flips me the other one. He saunters to his end of the court as if he has just said nothing particularly interesting.

I stand, staring at him, even though I know, intellectually, I should be walking to the other end of the court. But, really.

"You played tennis, with Ronny frickin' Blue."

He has opened the can of balls, two-toned yellow and green. He bounces one, then another several times, hard, testing them out. He throws one down to where I'm supposed to be, puts one into his pocket, then bounces the other one intensely.

"Yeah," he says, addressing the ball. "It's tennis. I'll play with anybody."

I walk to my end of the court, not looking at him but still talking to him. "You are going to tell me the rest of this story, are you not?"

"Excellent idea," he says when we're faced up to each other like real tennis players. "We'll play for info bits. Like points. Every time you score, I gotta give you a detail."

We never even keep score. We just hit back and forth, and it's fun, and it's exhausting. Great sweaty exercise, and soothingly simple.

"And when you score?" I say wearily.

"Umm, let's see. Okay, how's this? We'll keep score like a regular tennis game, fifteen, thirty, forty, game. Only we'll use letters. *J*, *U*, *N*, *E*, and when I win, you have to step aside and let me ask her out. Deal?"

"Well, hey, that sounds like a pretty good deal. But you should also consider these other two options. I could beat you to death with a tennis racket. Or we could just hit back and forth for a while and you can talk or shut up however much you like."

He waves his racket like a surrender, holds the ball up, preparing to serve.

"I'll take option three there," he says as he launches a serve my way.

We are good at this. I had almost forgotten how good we are at this. Not tennis per se, although I'm not bad at it and Malcolm is well above average. But the tennis talk, tennis tit for tat that always evolved from one of these sessions and caught us up on things no matter how out of touch we'd been.

"Your serve is still sharp," I say right after smacking one into the net.

"I told you," he says, raising another ball, "I still play all the time." *Thwack.*

"Right"—*thwack*—"with Ronny Blue."

"Among others." *Thwack.*

We rally for quite a while now, and this is when I like it best and it reminds me of what I have missed without realizing I missed it. We hit stride, and the rhythm of our baseline returns is musical and soothing and exciting all at once. He's using his superior skill to make sure I get balls I can return cleanly, and I return the favor by returning them.

I had missed a lot of life, I think, while I was lost in June. Maybe now I will start getting it back.

Though I'd just as soon not.

"So, Mal, you gonna tell me about the Ronny Rat connection or continue to jerk me around?"

"I'd really prefer to jerk you around for a while more, if you don't mind."

"I don't mind," I say. And I don't. Because for a guy who's jerking another guy around, he doesn't seem to be enjoying it all that much. And because the resulting wordlessness is making our scuffling, thwacking tennis sounds all the richer. Malcolm and my parents and whoever else was involved in arranging this were right. This is a kind of tonic for me.

After a rally of about fifty consecutive shots each, I put another one into the net. As I retrieve it, I feel talk is once again appropriate, at least the kind of meaningless chatter that used to be the fuel of these breezy warm long afternoons. "Did you hear that One Who Knows won the lottery. Again," I say.

"That's the rumor," he says.

"Rumor? Malcolm, don't you know that with One Who Knows there are no rumors? Have you ever heard a rumor about that guy that turned out not to be true?"

I am standing at the net now, like I've come up for a volley, and I can see an unexpected seriousness on his face.

"I suppose," he says enigmatically. "I hope not. Maybe not."

I stare at him. He shrugs. I go back to my baseline.

I serve. Into the net. I serve. Long, but returnable. We rally again. Then he does some blurting among the hitting.

"I asked her out."

"What?"

We keep hitting, keep talking.

"I asked her out."

"No."

"Yes."

We start hitting harder.

"And?"

"She said okay."

I hit one really hard. Over the twelve-foot fence and everything. Malcolm starts to retrieve it.

"Don't!" I shout. "Get back there. Use the other ball."

He serves. We rally.

"So?" I say.

"So I went over to her house. That's when I met Ronny. Started talking about tennis. Turns out he's a keen tennis player and—"

"I don't care about you and Ronny and tennis!" I shout, missing one return completely, then picking up a ball and throwing it at Malcolm. Then in a fit of inspiration I throw my racket at him too. It bounces to a landing at his feet.

"You did say you wanted to know—"

"That was before. Nothing else matters now!"

He is walking—very bravely, under the circumstances— toward me at the net with my racket. Even more bravely, he is grinning at me.

"Malcolm," I say in the kind of supercalm voice that only ever seems to come out of people going criminally insane, "there are very few matters in life that are genuinely life-or-death, but explaining that smirk to me right now is surely one of them."

"Dammit, boy, if your love-puppy thing isn't a sight to behold," he says, handing my racket across as either a peace offering or suicide.

"Which makes you twice as evil for trying to tear it up."

"First, I wasn't tearing anything up, since you were already split. Second, I had no idea your precious love was quite as spectacularly pathetic as this. Third, the joke was on me all along, as it turned out she agreed to see me just to get updates on you. Which I didn't even have, so I guess the joke was on her as well. And I suppose, from the cross-eyed mental on your face right now, the joke was on you, too, although you appear not to see the funny."

I somehow *missed* Malcolm's company?

"So, Mal, if you already asked Junie out, and in fact sort of did go out with her, what's with all the asking my permission?"

"Well, I had a guilt attack. And while it all ended innocently enough, and she was clearly still into you, and remember you did dump me and all, I still felt like I needed to sort of make good. You know, like when a guy puts an extension on his house without getting permits, then applies for them retroactively so that he doesn't get into any trouble. This is me retroactively eliminating any trouble. So, that's that, then. Want to go to a movie tonight or hit the amusement park for old times' sake?"

I feel like I'm already at the amusement park, old times or not. Head is rattling, stomach swirling like I'm on the Tilt-a-Whirl for the first time again.

I find myself staring at the tennis racket in my hands, turning it over and over.

"I'm not even sure if I'm supposed to hit you now," I say.

"I don't think you are," he says.

"Maybe later, then. You're confusing me so much right now that I have to reserve the right to come to my senses and clock you one later."

"Of course, of course," he says, then reaches across the net and slaps me on the neck. He leaves his hand there and squeezes. "You two are awfully cute. Weird as shit, as far as couples go. But damn cute. Why'd you break up, anyway?"

"I wish I knew. From the sound of it you probably know more about it than I do. What did she say, anyway?"

"Are we done playing?" he asks.

Knowing how hard it can be to get a focused story out of Malcolm when he is not swinging a racket, I push him in the direction of his own baseline.

"Serve," I say. And I know he knows I mean more than a fuzzy yellow ball.

Not that there were a million details to be learned from the great date, but what was there was enough to put a little lift in my heart, and to prompt me to have him repeat a couple of choice moments three times.

"Sounds like she likes me better now than when we were together," I say.

"Yeah," he responds with a small chuckle. "I'd say you guys are in great shape."

"What am I going to do, Mal?" I ask. I'm sitting cross-legged at the net, looking up at him as he does a decent job of juggling two tennis balls with one hand.

"That's a very good question, O. Are you not still planning to go into your dad's business?"

I was never planning on going into my dad's business, because I was never *planning* on going into anything at all. I've been short of anything one might call direction during the whole period when my peers and classmates have been finding their callings one by one. College, military, trades, crime, it seemed like everybody I knew had it figured; good, bad, but not a single one indifferent. Except me.

"I was never planning on going into Dad's business, Mal. And anyway I wasn't even asking about that. I meant about—"

"College?"

Malcolm is going to college. He never had any doubt.

"I meant Junie, man."

"Oh, she's planning to go to college. But she's taking a year off first. To work and save some money. She wants to go away. Far, far away, like multiple state lines. Not me, though. Plenty of fine schools within laundry and pot roast distance of home, is how I've always seen it."

"Is it juggling, Malcolm, that does this to your brain? Because you're telling me a whole load of stuff, stuff that I already know, stuff that you already know I know, and stuff—more important—that I never even asked you about."

He lets the balls drop and bouncety-bounce on the ground between us. He stares at me.

"I think it probably is the juggling, man. I'm with you now, though."

"Thanks. I'm talking about Junie. Where she is. Where we are. And, literally, where she *is*."

"To be honest, I don't know the answers to any of that. To be also honest, maybe you need to stop obsessing about Junie Blue and just get on with stuff. Like figuring out what you're gonna do with the next critical phase of life. Junie will be fine, man. She's as tough as nails and hotter than the sun's ass, and if there is a more winning combination than that, I would like to know where it can be purchased. You, on the other hand, are currently lacking in dynamism."

It's true enough. I am lacking in dynamism. It's also true that Junie is hard and together and probably a whole lot less in need of me than I am in need of being needed—so, what, honestly, am I worried about?

Myself, maybe?

"Let's go home, Mal," I say.

"What?" he says when I hop to my feet in a burst of negative dynamism. He follows me off the courts, and we head up the road together. "Did I say something wrong? Are you going to banish me from your life again?"

"I never banished you. And I'm sorry. It won't happen again."

"Cool. Though, come Labor Day you're gonna be the banished one when I head off to college. Unless you come with me. Come with me."

I could. We were accepted to the same college, and we both accepted our acceptances. The difference is, Malcolm always intended to go, and I just needed something to show my parents to keep them from talking too much about what I was going to do. It wasn't a wildly successful plan, since I don't think it fooled anybody. But still, it's there.

"We'll see," I say.

"You know, O, you're not really believable even when you're trying. And that one was just lifeless."

We both laugh at my lameness. Then he drifts behind and sticks the butt of his racket into the small of my back like a gun.

"Come on, you," he demands, "make a move. Or else."

I almost wish it were as simple as a shotgun life.

We walk more or less like this all the way back to my place. Not the gun-in-my-back part, but still in the style of escorted prisoner. I don't know what's in it for him—a laugh, probably—but for me it serves the purpose of allowing me to be on my own without being alone. Good man, Malcolm.

"Thanks, man," I say, pivoting in front of my house in a crisp, military way that says clearly there will be no invitation inside. Even though he deserves one. Even though I could really use him. "I had fun."

"Yeah," he says. "Fun. It's written all over your face." He points at my face, in case I've forgotten where it is.

"Really?" I say.

"No," he says. "You look like flaming crap, Oliver."

That's crossing a Rubicon there. Even my parents almost always call me O, or Son, or something like that. If I get called by my actual name once every six days, that's going at quite a clip, and since Malcolm hasn't been around, the clip has been clipped to nearly nothing at all. It always means something when he uses it, even if I rarely know exactly what that something is.

"I don't," I say with exactly the conviction a flaming-crap face would give it.

He puts all the tennis gear down, right there on the sidewalk, where any old type of harm could come to his precious racket—also a blue-moon occurrence. He puts both hands heavily on my shoulders.

"Go inside. Watch a movie. Eat. Have a bath. Google yourself. Google yourself until you go blind, in fact. Then change the sheets, have another bath, or maybe a shower this time. Then get some real sleep. You need a shave and a haircut. *Don't* do those things for yourself. Tomorrow a.m. I'll come by and we'll go get buffed up, all right? Sound good? All right?"

I'm thinking about all the various constituent parts of that plan, or at least I'm trying to think of the various constituents.

"All right," I say.

But truth is, all I can hear inside is *Junie Blue, Junie Blue, Junie Blue, Junie Blue* echoing like a cuckoo's call around the vast forest of my skull.

Mal collects up his stuff and walks off silently.

"Thank you so much, Malcolm," comes the whisper-voice from behind the screen.

"Jesus, Mom!" I snap, and march inside.

Four

Malcolm was right about my being pathetic.
He must have been. Otherwise why would I have gone into the house and followed his instructions to the letter? Most of them, anyway, as I was pretty tired and too distracted to be really up to much.

"Appearance is half your problem, O," he says as we turn onto Ocean Boulevard. "Maybe even more than half."

"Is that so?" I say.

"That is so. Trust me, you're gonna be a new man after this. Then you can dispose of that old man you got going there, because he frankly stinks."

"So, a trip to Santo's is going to change everything?"

"Everything."

This is a remarkably bold claim, since not only has this establishment had previous opportunities to make a new man of me, but it is as responsible as any other place in the world for the me that I already am. On the outside, that is.

I got my first ever haircut at Santo's. I don't remember it, but I know this to be true, because I got all of my haircuts here, and the first haircut I do remember, I was maybe four years old and Santo himself hauled out this wooden plank and laid it across the arms of the barber chair to make a booster seat because even with the chair pumped up as high as it could go, the old duffer still had to stoop to clip me.

And an old duffer he was. Santo was an old man when I was four and twelve and fifteen, until he retired or whatever it was he did, but it didn't matter because he always worked side by side with another old guy just like him—and two or three rotating other old guys when times were good and all four chairs were buzzing. Then he retired or whatever it was and he was replaced by another Santo, and it was like there was this workshop someplace where they just turned out replicate barber Santos, which suited everybody fine.

And the place was never actually called Santo's, because it was and still is officially called the Beachcomber Gentleman's Barbershop. Perfectly named. Great big front windows as big as the mirror wall, and if you look to your right from one of the chairs, you get the most spectacular view of the beach, and if you look to your right to see the beach while getting your hair cut, Santo would always sharply grab the point of your chin and whip you back around to proper haircuttee position.

Almost everybody who came into the place had sand in his hair, especially on a windy day, and this is possibly why all the combs and clippers and hair tonics and whatever Santo would attack you with always had the grittiness.

A gritty kind of place, to be sure.

Because the smells of sand and salt and the seaside stuff and the smells of the barber business, circa 1927, always swirled together in the atmosphere of Santo's in such a reliable balance as to suggest somebody on staff was tasked with the job of creating exactly this olfactory singularity. Singular. It exists nowhere else, I am certain.

Also gritty because that's how Santo's sees itself. A little bit dangerous, a little bit fringes-of-society atmosphere is part of the charm of the place. Even if it's not entirely believable, not always charming.

"Heya, kid," the old guy says, springing out of his chair on a quiet Monday morning.

We're all kids and we always will be. Kid, kidnik, kiddo, regardless. It was this way with the original Santo, and it is this way with Santo IV or whoever we have here.

"The kids, kid and kiddo," he says, just as happily as if we were his actual grandchildren coming to see him for the first time in a year.

"Hey, Santo," Malcolm says, giving the old boy a big hug. "I saw you, sitting there staring out at the waves."

"Of course I was staring out at the waves. They're waves, for cryin' out loud. They're frickin' beautiful. Does that make me a bad person? I don't think that makes me a bad person. First customers of the week, you kids. Sure I stare at the waves. Gets me in the mood, in the spirit, so I can do my best work. For you. All for you."

"Hey, and we appreciate it. That's why we come back, right?"

"Right," he says. "And what are we in for today?"

I step up. Malcolm points at me with his thumb.

"Kiddo," Santo says, taking me by the arm like I'm the little old guy and he is helping me into the chair, "how did you let it get like this?"

Malcolm laughs out loud, throws himself into a chair with a newspaper and a good angle to see me in the mirror.

Santo does this thing—I suppose the same thing a sculptor does when he starts on a project. He clips, a tiny bit, a nothing bit, then steps back and looks. Goes to a whole other part of the head, snips a clip, steps back, looks, tilts his head, looks, comes back in for more. Like he is waiting for the proper image to suggest itself to him, to emerge from the chaos that is my currently configured head.

I forgot how long this takes.

The step-backs get less frequent, the clippings more so, and something like progress is happening when the bell over the door clinks and I see the men swagger in.

They are a type. Junie always hated it when I saw things

this way, so I stopped talking about it mostly, although I never quite stopped thinking it. Types. A type. All three men are big guys, two big-bigs and a short big, and all have suits on. Middle aged. Slicked hair, big rings, neck and wrist chains. Cologne. Dear lord, the cologne. Colognes. It's the cologne wars as the guys' scents fight it out for the air space as they take up three wall seats next to Malcolm, and then the colognes join forces to defeat all the old-timey barber aromas, and pretty much wipe out the beach smells entirely.

"Whew," Santo says to the guys, pausing just to make the *Phew* wave in front of his nose with his scissors hand. "What'd you boys, swim here through a sea of Avon ladies?"

"Harrr-hahahahaha," the boys all howl. Good-time boys. They like to laugh. They love a laugh and they love to be the subjects of a good gag that doesn't cut too close but doesn't miss their specialness either. A type. Junie would kill me. Malcolm laughs, long and loud. He's a different type.

The three men talk in loud voices, about what they read in the day-old newspapers and month-old magazines they pick up off the seats. Like the long line of Santo barbers, these guys have been here and have been doing this for forever. They rarely get haircuts, occasionally shaves, but their presence is as much a part of the place as the swirling barber pole out front.

Malcolm waves at me in the mirror, shakes his head and

rolls his eyes at the men. I wave back, raising my hand under the big nylon bib, causing the whole thing to tent up and send hairs sliding away to the floor. Santo slaps my hand back down. Malcolm laughs.

Suddenly the whole thing feels so melancholy, I don't know what I'll do. It comes over me in a wave, and really, I'm so blindsided by it, I don't have a response for it, for me.

It's Junie, of course. It's her. And everything. What am I doing here, in the barbershop of my whole life? What am I grooming for? I'm supposed to be high-diving into big life right about now, but I'm . . .

I'm what? I don't even know that?

But I do know that if I let what wants to happen happen and I start getting all misty-faced here, I will be skinned like a fish by the crowd, by the old pal, and by the barber himself. When I cried once in this chair, I was certain from the look that Santo was going to beat me up. And I was four.

I look to my right, out the window, out past the thrilling crashing waves and the infinite potential sea. This, this is better.

Santo whips me by the chin tip back in the direction of the mirror with such force that my eyes don't focus again for three or four seconds. When they do, I see Malcolm laughing again. Santo squints and resumes intensely sculpting me back to respectability. As he finishes the right side of my head and works his way around back, I gradually let myself rotate in the direction of the beach again. The place that's always there for me. All the elements combine just so to re-right me when I breathe it in, take it in.

Only, something's in the way.

Ronny Blue is standing there, all wide-boy wide stance, wide grin as he stares in the window and into me.

"Ronny Blue, Blue Ronny!" comes the triumphant call of the masses as Ronny comes through the door.

"Hello there, boys," Ronny says as he swaggers in. He stands there, in front of the row of chairs, as the men all burble greetings and gentle ass-kisses. Malcolm—my Malcolm—actually rises to his feet, goes to shake the great man's hand.

"Are you *kidding* me?" I blurt as Malcolm anxiously waves me off.

"Hey, why ain't we out playing tennis, a day like this?" Ronny bellows as if Malcolm were in another barbershop two towns away.

"I don't know, Ronny. Why aren't we?" he answers.

Malcolm stands there, stupid, as if he expected a real answer, and is left to look as foolish as he deserves when Ronny just walks away to come and greet Santo.

"Santo, my brother, how are we doin' today?" Ronny says, slapping my well-armed haircutter firmly on the shoulder of his clipping hand.

"Ouch," I snap, feeling at the spot behind my ear that isn't bleeding on the outside but might as well be.

"Santo," Ronny says, mock-scolding, "be careful. You gotta go extra easy on these delicate rich boys. They ain't like you and me."

Sigh. It's going to be like this.

"What are you doing here in my neighborhood, in my shop, anyway?" Ronny says as he leans right into my face with a polished fun-house smile bearing down on me.

His neighborhood, his shop.

The town is shaped roughly like a backward capital letter *N*, with an additional line drawn straight across the top. That additional line across the top would be the beach boulevard and, obviously, the beach. The right-hand leg of the backward *N* would basically be my section of town, with the left-hand leg being Junie's. The diagonal connecting them is a gradually progressing gradation of tone from their harder-edged neighborhood to my, I suppose, more affluent one. A color chart from Blue to me.

The beach is nobody's. It's everybody's. It's practically the one thing that everyone understands.

Everyone except Ronny Blue, apparently. But there are lots of things that he doesn't understand.

"Funny, Ronny," I say, "I always thought this place belonged to Santo."

Ronny straightens up, turns his backside to me in the rudest manner imaginable, and then addresses me in the mirror. He taps an index finger to the side of his nose, indicating his knowing hush-hush insiderism and *Shut up, Junior* warning. God, do I hate that gesture.

Santo says nothing. Goes back to clipping me.

Ronny throws himself roughly into the one remaining observation chair, the one closest to the door.

"Imagine," he says, folding his hands, all piety and admiration. "The likes of him, coming all the way down here to drop his hairs on our floor. Hey, maybe we can collect them up and sell them to tourists. Or maybe give them to the local poor, like, what do them people do again, sell them like holy water or Mary's tears or pieces of that cross thing, huh? The upper classes, man, do they ever stop giving?"

"I'm not upper anything," I say weakly.

This is so uncomfortable. There cannot have ever been a less relaxing haircut in the history of scissors. And I look up, realize that Santo, working at the speed of Santo, is still less than half-done with me. Ronny glares, grins, and scowls all at once and makes sure there is no doubt he is staring bullets into my eyes and has every intention of continuing to do so.

"What about tomorrow, Ronny?" Malcolm asks, and I could personally give him a free all-over baldy haircut right now. What is it about low-level criminality that makes certain posh boys want to roll in it like a dog with a dead thing?

"Maybe," Ronny says flatly without releasing me from his stare.

It's killing me, and I'm pretty sure he knows it.

I turn to my ally, the ocean. Santo whips my head back. The sudden loss of eye focus is actually rather pleasant. The bite of the pinched nerve in my neck, less so.

You cannot let this happen. If you let the bully bully, then you'd better learn to love the bullying. You've got to give it *something*.

I stare as hard as my watery eyes will allow, right back into him.

"Junie back from her vacation yet?"

Momentarily, deliciously, he looks startled. Then he comes back, leaning hard and mean into the task.

"What vacation?" he says, hands outstretched, looking down the line of sycophants, playing to the mob.

Through gritted teeth I venture further into what already looks like an unfortunate dialogue.

"The vacation she was on when I came to your house."

"What?" he says, all cartoon surprise. "You was at my house? Jeez, I gotta get a dog."

His fans don't let him down, and the place rocks with enough rumbling laughter that Santo has to pause for the tremor to pass.

Ronny's stupid, but he's winning.

"Did she come home yet, Ronny?" I snap.

"What, home? She was never away." He looks to the flunkies again. "She was there all the time, just didn't want to see this schmuck."

They are falling all over one another. I look at my pal Malcolm, to see him very diplomatically giving me sympathy eyes and a shrug through his own complicit laughter.

I'm boiling now. I see my face in the mirror like an angry red sunset. "Liar," I say.

It's all going so well for him, he's not even insulted.

"All too true, I'm afraid, sonny. She was right down the hall, in her room. But she had a bunch of guys in there and a 'Do Not Disturb' sign on the door."

"Shut up, Ronny."

"I think it was a basketball team. They were tall, anyway."

"That's your daughter, you animal."

"Hey, how do you think *I* feel? I thought you were bad, but it's just gotten worse and worse. She doesn't have any quality control at all at this point. You were the beginning of the end, I think."

Getting louder didn't help me, so despite his rollicking crowd support, I decide to go for quieter.

"You have no shame, Ronny Blue, you know that?"

"What? Haven't you been listening? I got plenty of shame.

I'm rotten with shame. I got shame comin' out the wazoo. I mean, if she did even *this* guy, how low could she go?"

It's all swim now. I don't need to look out to the ocean for help, because the ocean has come right in here to do the job. It feels like the shop has filled right up to the ceiling, with rich, salty, sting-y seawater and we are all floating in it. I stare, squint, lean in the direction of Malcolm's cloudy, distant reflection, and can only half-hear him over the din, or through the water, as he says slowly, "No, no, no, no," his lips mouthing, *"No, no, no, no,"* and he looks like a damn fish.

"Where is sheeeeee?" I scream, out of my mind, giving Ronny Blue exactly the gift he's been snuffling for, giving his fans just the performance they paid for.

"She's at work, you idiot," he snarls.

I leap out of the chair, out of astonished Santo's grasp. I tear off the bib, stick some bills into his hand.

"There he goes, giving to the poor again," Ronny says.

I dash for the door, and just as I get there, the big man himself is on his feet, blocking my way. My nose comes just about to Ronny's lips.

True venal wickedness has a smell all its own.

After he has held me, wordlessly, effortlessly, right there for his chosen number of seconds, he sits back down. Malcolm comes up behind me as I open the door, until Ronny puts out a hand. "We need to talk about tennis," he says to Malcolm, and like that, I am running on my own.

If you closed your eyes while making the journey from my house to Junie's, or mine to the beach to Junie's, you would know at every step where you were. The air is different. The beach, of course, is all the things the beach is supposed to be—salt and sand and fried clams and sugar and Coppertone and crabs opened belly-up on the pasted low-tide mudflats. But you could also smell the difference between mine and Junie's. Drier down my way, greener, pine jostling with honeysuckle and roses. Junie's you can smell as you cross that invisible line, between here and there, between this and that. There is a moisture there that we don't seem to have, rich oils, spice, air that is heavier than what hangs around my house.

I am sweating and breathing heavily as I reach the corner shop where she works. That is due to the exertion of getting myself here without wasting a single second more, but I'd be sweating and hyperventilating even if somebody'd hauled me in a rickshaw.

I really need to see her.

I burst through the big glass door with all the gusto of an armed robber.

"Dammit hell, O!" Junie shouts when she realizes she is not being robbed.

"Well, dammit hello to you, too," I say, and I know I am being maybe a tad too wise guy for the level of her actual fright, but I cannot contain myself. I would bet my heart is pounding two-to-one against hers, I am so ridiculously pumped to see her.

There is nobody else in the small shop at the moment, and it feels very much like old times as I walk up to the counter and reach over to put my hand on her hand.

It is very much new times when she says flatly, "What are you doing here?"

"I came to see you," I say helpfully.

"But why would . . . ," she says, then switches directions as she scans up at my current look. "What's going on with your head?" she says, bursting out laughing.

I reach up to the spot she appears to be focused on, the side of my head that just got groomed.

"Oh," I say, "I was just at Santo's."

"I guess nobody ever told Santo not to run with those scissors, because he appears to have put one of his eyes out."

"Ha. Jeez, I missed you. Where you been?"

"Are you telling me that's an actual haircut? My god, what did I do to you when I dumped you?"

I am so easily wounded. I hate, damn, hate that I am so easily wounded.

"Don't say that, huh, Junie?"

"Sorry, O." She pauses, looking at me apprehensively. "You mean about the dumping, or the stupid haircut?"

"Ah, the dumping."

"Cool. So, what about the hair?"

"The hair is because I jumped right out of Santo's chair when I heard you were here. Couldn't even wait to get finished—"

"I hear he takes a long time."

"Cripes, it's endless. So I couldn't wait once I heard."

"What's the big deal? This is where I work. I'm here a lot."

"Well, your father told me that—"

"That scuzzbag."

"Indeed, that scuzzbag."

"What did he tell you?"

"That you were here."

"Okay. Once again, not headline news, O."

"Well, it was after all the other stuff he said."

She waits, but not long.

"Okay, *Oliver*? I don't know which is bothering me more right now, that haircut or the maddening way you are telling me details, but one way or another I am going to take a pair of scissors to your head if you don't get to it."

I take a deep breath. I'm sure, subconsciously, I was talking so roundabout because I didn't really want to repeat what the scuzz was saying, as I am ordinarily fairly straight-forward. I exhale.

"He said you were having sex with a basketball team."

She stares at me, completely coldly.

"Did he say which team?"

I stare at her, completely coldly.

"Don't be a numbnuts, O."

I nod frantically. "Right, right, sorry." I try to be all cool now. "So, that means you didn't, right?"

She stops even looking at me. She walks around from behind the counter, goes to a hanging display, a panel on the wall that holds an array of household items like nail clippers and sewing stuff, the kind of things you would always buy at a big normal store unless you had an emergency, in which case you get them at a place like this. She pulls down a pair of grooming shears and rips the package right open.

"Right, you," she says, and she presses the point of the shears into my cheek with a surprising amount of push. It hurts. She never does anything lightly, Junie Blue.

She grabs me by the shirt and tugs me around to the other side of the counter, stuffs me roughly down onto the stool she was sitting on, and commences improving me.

Just like ever.

She clips, she leans, she looks, she clips, she knows. Junie is the anti-Santo, sure and deliberate, confident enough in what she's doing that I don't need a mirror to feel handsome in her hands.

"Do you love me?" I ask. She loves me when I'm provocative.

"Do you love your eyes?" she asks, poised to gouge. I love her menacing.

And yes, I love my eyes. Love them more sometimes than others. Love them more right now than ever. Her reddish brown hair hangs straight to her shoulders, bangs draping almost to her fair, clearly touched-up eyebrows. She's got on that orange lipstick I adore—*Creamsicle*, not orange—and her puffy lips look more pillowy than ever. I often asked her why she bothered with makeup, and she replied that that is why I would never see her without makeup. We only dated the last year-plus of school, but I cannot recall a time before I felt about her the way I feel about her right this minute.

"I want you to cut my hair all the time."

"No."

"Where were you this weekend?"

"None of your business."

"I heard something about you and Malcolm."

"Yeah, well, I heard you were bangin' my sister."

"What? Where did you ever—"

"That's the rumor mill for ya, O. Live by it, die by it.

What kind of haircut do you want in the end here, the kind powered by rumors or the good kind?"

"Good, please," I say, and she smiles softly, returning to the clipping. A pair of elderly women come in. One picks up a basket, and they begin working their way around the shop. June keeps one eye on my hair and the other—

"Is your eye swollen?" I say abruptly, because I realize it is, and with a bit of uncommon fluid redness in the outside corner.

"No, it isn't, but how would you like your eye—"

"Knock it off, Junie. Not this time. What happened to your eye?"

She calmly goes on clipping, surely nearing the end now.

"I have two answers for you, O. Nothing. And none of your business."

The ladies come to the counter, start piling up their groceries. Canned vegetables and boxed soups, two green bananas, a half gallon of strawberry ice cream from a dairy I thought folded when I was in grade school, and a *TV Guide* magazine.

Junie hands me the scissors. "Here, finish yourself off," she says slyly.

"And two of those scratch tickets," one of the ladies says.

Junie reaches around right in front of me to peel two tickets off the roll, and from this angle I see another new something I don't like. It's a big red burn mark, circular, about the size of a quarter, in the middle of the back of her hand.

I grab her wrist. She reaches with the free hand and gives my hand such a sharp wallop that the clap fills the shop and I get stares of shock from both of the customers. Smoothly Junie swings back in their direction and closes the transaction.

When the shoppers have left, Junie turns back in my direction. I am sitting, stupid, in the chair, staring up at her, while she leans back, half-sitting on the counter.

It is a cool, hard stare-off, and I never, not once, came close to bettering her in one of these. Junie Blue could make the head on a coin blink first.

"So," I say finally, "where did you—"

"Change the subject or get out, O. I'm not kidding."

Getting out right now sounds like the most awful thing.

"You sell a lot of lottery tickets, huh?" I say, feeling like I am trying desperately to make conversation for the first time with this wonderful girl.

"They carry the shop."

"Huh, interesting," I say, uninterested. "Is it true that Juan won again? Rumor has it, you know."

"Rumor can have *this*," she says, making an obscene gesture that would likely make her father weep with pride.

We stare at each other a little more, until the door opens

again, to a gaggle of unruly kids who must be the scourge of little shops like this.

"You should probably go now," she says, with none of the harshness at all.

I nod, stand up. "Why are we not together, Junie?"

"Because that's the way I want it." Again, the hard words and the soft delivery have no business in the same room together.

"I think maybe you need me, though," I say.

She snags the scissors out of my hand, and the hard words join up with the hard delivery in a perfectly synchronized, "Get. Out."

I am walking quickly around the counter toward the door when she calls me back. I race toward her, only to find her palm outstretched and waiting.

"You owe me," she says, "for the haircut. I'm a working-class gal, and I need to get paid."

"Of course," I say, "of course." I fish some crinkly bills out of my pocket, from which she selects something fair. She was always fair with me, before the unfairness.

I head out again, until she calls me back with a barking, "Hey."

All the kids stop to watch now, and they *oooh* a little as I trudge back to the reckoning.

"We sell stuff here."

"I'm aware of that."

"Well, did that brand-new scissors climb down off the rack and unpackage itself?"

I am not even a little bit curious about what will result if I take up the obvious dare and point out that she opened the scissors, not I. I pay up. She hands over the scissors, and it feels more like a last laugh than a fair trade.

I am aware of the low-level murmuring of kids mocking me as I finally make the door. But it is nothing compared to Junie's farewell.

"I *need* you?" she says, and laughs, growls at my back.

Five

"You paid for this haircut?" my mother says, laughing, walking around and around me as I sit in the chair.

"Twice," I say, surrendering completely.

She continues circling, looking for a way in. "This is clearly the work of a woman scorned."

"I didn't scorn anybody," I say. "She's killing me, Mom. She really is."

There is a voice coming through the window screen where my mother usually hangs out. "Hello? Hello?" It's Malcolm.

"Speaking of killing," I say, jumping up just as my mother takes her first remedial clip at my temple.

"That was very dangerous," she says.

I run down the hallway to the front room, where I throw down to my knees with enough force to make both kneecaps crunch and shift out of place.

I am face-to-face with Malcolm on the other side of the screen. Our noses are practically pressed to each other.

"I am going to kick your ass," I say.

"No, you're not," he says.

"And why not?"

"Because you and I are not men of violence, that's why not."

"I am now a man of violence," I assure him, "and you are a man of getting his ass kicked."

"The whole neighborhood can hear you," Mom calls.

I drop my voice, which I was about to do at this point anyway.

"Did you do it with Junie, Malcolm?"

"No."

"Tell me the truth."

"The truth?"

"The truth."

"I'll tell you the truest truth I know. And that is, people lie. Everybody lies."

"Not everybody."

"Of course, everybody."

"You?"

"Of course me. Everybody."

"So. Are you lying? Did you do it?"

"Did you really sleep with Maxine?" he asks. "That is so awesome."

Mom calls from the other room again. "I think I want to sketch you before I fix that hair, if you don't mind."

Malcolm points at my head and offers me some unnecessary advice. "Dude, *mind*."

It is all getting the better of me. I used to think lying was a great lark, back when I brilliantly thought I was the only one doing it. Or, one of the two.

Lyin' O'Brien.

Sweet Junie Blue Lies.

Life was sweet, and Blue, and just dubious enough.

"What are you here for, anyway, Malcolm?"

"Just wanted to see how you made out. You see June?"

"Yes, I saw June. What's it to you?"

"Jeez, testy."

"Did you do it, Mal?"

"No."

"Are you lying to me?"

"Do you mean right now, right this second?"

"That's what I mean."

"Then, no."

"Grrr."

"So what did you find out? From Junie?"

"What the hell are you going on about? What did I find out about what?"

Malcolm, for a change, goes silent. He points, with both index fingers, at a spot above and behind me. I turn to see my mother looming.

Chris Lynch

"Oliver can't come out to play right now, Malcolm," she says, tugging me to my feet by my ear.

"I'll call you," he says as I walk backward and he shrinks in the window frame. "We'll talk."

"Oh, what, about *tennis*?" I say, perhaps a little too sarcastically. There is more to him than that. "And your new tennis *pal*?"

"Or about Maxie Blue?" he says leeringly.

"Or not," I say.

"Okay, about Junie Blue," he says.

"Or about my kicking your ass blue," I say, and my mother yanks my ear sharply around the corner.

I wake up to a feeling of lightness I did not have the previous couple of days. I wake up, in fact, to a lightness I have not felt since the Split. I dreamed about her. But that's not unusual, so that's not it. It's more about the fact that the dream had a weave that it hasn't had before. It was threaded through by the thoughts I had before bed, and it is sustained now by the thought still living and bobbing and weaving this morning.

She needs me.

I am still worried about her, still scared as hell about what is going on.

But she needs me, and that's a start. I will not let her down.

It is with this lightness that I step into my clothes and head down the stairs with something like purpose, which has been howlingly absent from my first steps of recent days. I bop the last step, turn the corner into the kitchen.

Where I am blown right back into the hallway with the force of the voice.

"What have you been telling people!" Maxine screams.

"Nothing," I say, backing up as she walks forward. "I swear to you, nothing."

I'm not sure whether it's my genuine sincerity or my cowardly lion full-body tremble that does the trick, but she instantly dials it back.

"Okay," she says, nodding. "I didn't think it was you, but I had to ask. Sorry if I freaked you." She takes me by the hand and leads me toward my own dining room. She looks back at me, then down at my hand. "Ooh, shivering *and* sweaty. Be still my heart, manly man."

"Maxine, what are you doing here?"

"I'll show ya."

And show me she does.

"Leona?" I say to the lovely quiet lady at the table.

"Hello," she says, waving a small wave at me and almost giggling. Her smile is at least three times the volume of anything I ever saw her produce in her own home.

My mother is the picture of intense concentration. If she

looked halfway this focused when she drew me, I might not look like a salesman in the sketches for once.

"O," Mom says sweetly, "I have to tell you what a wonderful morning we are having here. "These women . . . are such a joy. I can't believe we are just getting to know one another like this now, after all this time. It's a shame it couldn't have happened before you and June had to split up. A real shame. I could draw these cheekbones all day."

Leona giggles.

"Yeah, I'm really sorry to have let everybody down and all. . . . Um, does Ronny know about this sitting?"

"Nnnnnope," Maxine says with more than a little delight. She offers me a green smoothie she apparently made in the kitchen without waking me. I take it. "The old ratpacker's got a birthday comin' up, and I'm giving him this as a present."

"Oh," I say. "Ah. Didn't he, though, make it really, really clear that he expected to be the one who got the first—"

"Yyyyyup," she says, then presses the blender high button and laughs kind of scarily over the gizmo's whine. "I could kill in that kitchen, by the way. It is amazing."

"On the subject of killing in the kitchen . . . any chance he follows your trail and winds up here this morning?"

"None at all. He's playing tennis with his new ball boy, your idiot friend. I tell you what, my old man might be a dope, but he can spot one of these preppy chumps a mile away and just makes a sport out of seeing how much he can get them to buff his boots, kiss his ass, lick—"

"Got it, Max. Your father is a crusader against the inequities of the class-based socioeconomic system we live in, and prides himself on redressing the situation in his own modest ways."

She gives me the devil's own smile, with devil's dimples. "I could not have put it one bit better."

I walk around behind my mother to glimpse the work at hand. I am stunned.

I like my mother's work. I love some of my mother's work, especially when I am not the subject. But there have been a few distinct occasions when her stuff has transcended . . . everything. However, while Leona is a strikingly pretty woman, she has always seemed to be carrying an extra ten pounds of face on her somehow, and it was striving to drag her right to the floor. Yet here, in this work right here in front of me, I see what I think is the more live-than-live-action Leona, more vibrant than any version of the real her I have seen. How, I wonder, is Mom doing that on their first ever meeting?

I look up, eventually, from the sketch to look at the model.

And I see. Leona, the flesh version, is giving off the same incandescence, the same vitality and just raw loveliness. I get actual, bumpy goose bumps as I look between model and drawing and model and I see the one feed the other and the other feed back the one.

Maxine hears me make some stupid grunt of approval and crowds right up next to me. She gets even more dazzled than me, more quickly.

"How," she says very deliberately, "is this done? It's like frickin' magic."

Mom can barely contain herself as she shifts side to side in her seat, blushes wildly, then looks up over her shoulder to see right into Maxine's upside-down face.

"I like to make the possible as possible as possible," says the artist. "When I can."

Maxine looks like she may even cry all over my mother. Then quietly says, "I cannot wait to see Ratass's fat face on his birthday."

So, a moment to warm all heart cockles.

It is ten thirty when it is deemed time for a work stoppage. Maxine, who completely owns this kitchen and dining room now, is serving coffee all around. Mom has instructed me to violate the dedicated Pepperidge Farm cupboard and plunk down a variety of those cookies they do like nobody's business. And because they are Pepperidge Farm cookies, they could just as easily be cakes or brownies or muffins as cookies and so are appropriate for any time of day.

The coffee, however, comes over smelling—in addition

to its fine, fine arabica tones—very suspicious indeed for ten thirty a.m.

I suspect Irish.

"Spanish, actually," Max says, passing them all around.

Nobody is registering any complaints.

After a bit the two moms are huddled over some of my mother's other sketches—far too many of me—and Max tugs me into the hallway and out to the backyard.

"So, I gotta ask," she says.

"Ask," I say.

"Does she got it?"

"Who got what?"

"Don't play stupid, O." She sips her coffee. "Does my sister have the damn lottery ticket?"

"What? I mean, what?" I sip my own coffee. It's awfully good. It might need to be stronger, though.

"Come on. I won't tell."

"Maxie, I don't know anything about this."

"Jeez, dummy, absolutely everybody is talking about it. Nobody's come forward to claim the winning ticket from last week. They know it was sold from a shop in our neighborhood. So you know One Who Knows considers it *his ticket*. If it was me, I'd give him the ticket and live off his underworld generosity for the rest of my lazy life. Sounds like a great deal to me. Most folks, though, even if they didn't think it was such a sweet arrangement, would still give him the ticket, out of fear of consequences. You'd have to be one stubborn, leather-ass lunatic to withhold, I figure."

As thoroughly chilling as I now find this discussion, I join Maxine in irresistible broad-bright grinning.

"Right," she says, pointing at me and clinking mugs of Spanish coffee. "Did somebody just say, 'Junie Blue'?"

I drink down my coffee, and that is that.

"This is serious, Maxie. Shit, this is serious."

"Could be it's not even her, since she's said nothing to me, or to you. Maybe it's just an honest oversight and she's not even involved. Maybe some old crock just has the ticket lodged in the crack of his crusty underwear someplace."

"Jesus, Max."

"Sorry, Mr. Sensitive. People are talking, however."

"She would have told you, though."

"O, she hides her *coffee* from me."

"Oliver," Mom calls from the other room.

When I get there, she and Leona are making plans for another sitting, more coffee, maybe some golf. The ladies have to be off so they can beat the beast home and not spoil the *surprise*. I'd bet he's not a fan of surprises. On the way to the door, Maxine and I exchange winks and knowing glances— and I don't even know what they mean.

What I do know is, I have to try.

"Wonderful people," Mom says as the door closes.

"Indisputably," I say, headed straight up the stairs.

"Where are you off to?"

"My room."

"Already? But you just came down. . . . Oh."

"Mom! Cripes. No."

I don't have time to address my tattered in-house repu-tation, as I must try to contact Junie. I dial her number, and it rings out. It does not even give me the opportunity to leave a message. I throw the phone onto the bed and start pacing.

I get a text message signal.

What? She snaps.

I return serve. *Do you have something to tell me?*

Yes. You're dumped.

You'd think that would get easier. Nope.

Where are you? Can I see you?

Bet you can if you squint and use your imagination.

Is there something wrong with me for sort of enjoying this?

Come on, Junie. This is hard.

At it again, are ya?

Right.

I phone her once more. She picks right up, laughing.

"I did forget how much fun that could be," she says.

"Good. So that's settled. We are back to being a fun couple."

"We're not, actually."

"Is it the basketball team?"

"Well, sure."

"Punch line? Please?"

"Um, no. Punch line is, just, no. Don't be a pain, O, huh? Please? I got things I need to do, for myself, that's all."

"I want to see you."

"I want to see you, too."

"Where are you?"

"Walking the dogs."

"That's not a place."

"Walking the dogs on the moon."

"Please?"

Pause.

"You gonna ask difficult questions and make a nuisance of yourself?"

I have to laugh. "Junie Blue, you know that our entire relationship was driven by exactly those things. Of course I am."

Click.

Desperately, frantically—which means I press one button and shake the phone like I'm strangling it—I try to call her back. It rings out, unanswered.

"Dammit, dammit, dammit," I say, strangling the phone and stomping all around my room. The phone's death rattle sounds, fortunately, just like my text alert.

Ipswich Street. The two big Boxer pups, so you better behave. Woof.

I am feeling altogether apprehensive but not altogether hopeless as I barrel down the stairs and out toward Ipswich.

Does a rotten-rich lottery winner walk other people's dogs?

"Does a rotten-rich lottery winner walk other people's dogs, numbskull?" Junie says as the one boxer, Yin, jerks her along the sidewalk.

"If it was me? No," I say as the boxer's brother, Yang, makes me look like a crash test dummy being dragged by a rope behind a car.

"Right. And so here I am, walking dogs like I always do, working the stupid corner store like I always do . . . and let's face it, like I probably always will do, in one form or another."

"Aw, you won't. Don't say that, Junie. You won't always."

She stops abruptly there on the sidewalk, staring hard at me to make her point. She opens her mouth to speak, and Yin yanks her hard, and the moment is less momentous. But she will not be denied her point.

"What if I am, though, huh? Oliver? What if this is me, and I settle into it and, so what? Huh? What if that?"

The hellhounds are working into a rhythm that is challenging but manageable, and the two of us struggle equally down the road, staring each other up and down as we do.

Seconds pass that should not pass. Seconds more pass as I realize this, and seconds more before I even try to make up for it.

"So what?" I say. "So what, so nothing. Great. If you are you and you do this forever, then excellent, as long as you are you."

I was dead before I got the first sentence out. She turns away from me, nodding, looking out over the lumpmuscle of dog ahead of her, and looking out beyond that, and whatever is beyond that.

"Okay," she says in an awful crush of a nowhere voice, and I could cut myself. "Okay, O."

"I mean it, Junie," I say.

"I know you do," she says. "I mean it too. I don't have the ticket. Maybe I sold it from the shop. And I hope it makes the poor stupid sonofabitch happy, I really do."

"Makes them and Juan happy," I say.

A fair amount of quiet time passes. We make a big circuit of the block. Each dog dumps. Junie picks up both, slapping my arm hard when I try to clean up after mine.

"Mine," she says. "They are *my* responsibility. And another thing," she adds, slamming the two heavy bags hard into the trash can, "if I did win that lottery, I wouldn't be passing that ticket on to that pocky old weasel, no way. Because if I won it, it would be *mine. Mine* matters. *Mine* matters as much as the money."

I don't respond, because response is not needed, not welcome, and I'm pretty sure not wise at the moment. We get to the door of Yin and Yang's owners, and Junie grabs the leash out of my hand.

"But—" I say as the two bruisers make every effort to pull her apart and away and down, but she manages somehow to not let any of it happen.

"Thanks," she says as she succeeds in wrangling them back inside, and I stand there staring at her absence for several long, long seconds.

That is the point at which Junie herself becomes a rumor to me. Calls go unanswered and unreturned. Texts likewise. I walk over to her shop two consecutive days, and on two consecutive days I lose the nerve to go inside, sensing that her wrath will not be preferable to her silence. I walk the streets where I know she has dog-walking arrangements, until I am certain the neighbors are keeping a diary of my suspicious movements.

I have to stop this. I have to stop. I need to move on. She doesn't need me. She doesn't need anybody. I am the one with needs. Beyond Junie Blue, I need . . . something. I am eighteen years old, it is hot summer now. The ocean is right there and the sky is right there and I want for nothing.

So what do I want?

I'm drifting. I know I'm drifting. Junie and Malcolm and the rest of the world seem to be getting on with things, but I don't even know what *things* are.

"Meet me for lunch."

It's my dad, and it's unusual. It is almost unheard of for him to be calling me in the middle of the workday, and it is utterly unprecedented for him to be asking me to lunch. Not that I couldn't go to lunch with him whenever or wherever I wanted to. I could. I've never tested it, but I'm sure I could. It's just that Dad doesn't really eat lunches, from what I can tell. He eats opportunity. That's what he says. He eats opportunity for lunch and burps dividends all afternoon.

"Really?" I say warily.

"Sure. It'll be fun."

"Fun? Okay, I like fun."

"Sure you do. Everybody likes fun. See you at one."

I hang up, stare at my phone, not sure it actually did what it just did.

Message beep comes ten minutes later as I shave.

Make it 1:45. Fun!

Fun!

The restaurant is amazing, right around the corner from Dad's office. We are on, like, the fiftieth floor, looking out over the financial district and the port beyond and the rest of the world beyond that. It's a twenty-five-minute train ride from our town to down here, or a thirty-five-minute car ride in traffic. Dad likes driving.

"How do you like it?" Dad says without indicating whether it is the obscenely lush menu, the view, the cold red draft beer he ordered for himself and then slipped to me, or the buttery cubed steak appetizers with three different kinds of dips that just arrived. Not that it matters.

"Phenomenal, Dad," I say.

"Could eat here every day, couldn't you?"

"I could if I wanted to have gout and diabetes and heart trouble," I say.

"True. Well observed. You are a quick study, my lad. You know, there's also a fantastic gym in my building. Pool, sauna, and everything. So, you could eat here every day and *still* avoid all that."

"Having it all, huh, Dad?"

"Yep, kid, having it all. Or you could just eat opportunity for lunch every day, thereby having it all . . . and then some. All is nothing. Someday you'll look at having it all as underachieving."

"I can't work down here, Dad."

"Oop, sounds to me like someone needs another delicious illegal beverage."

I laugh. He makes me laugh pretty much at will, and

always has. It's one of his superpowers, possibly his most deadly one, and the one I need to ward against the most.

"Listen, Dad, you are awesome at what you do. I could never in a million years get to the point where—"

"One afternoon," he says, coolly taking a sip of his ice water with a straw. He loves his ice water with a straw, and it makes him look instantly boyish and innocent.

"What?"

"I could teach you everything I know in an afternoon. We'd still have time for a round of golf—which I will also need to teach you—before dinner."

"I know how to golf, Father."

"Aw, that's cute. Anyway, the business side of the business. Here's one of the main things about success, especially in my field, but it applies in every field of endeavor: Will trumps skill. Understand me? If you are willing, if you are driven, if you are prepared to do what it takes when you find out what it takes, you are going to mop the floor with the guys who have the skill without the will."

"Huh," I say, genuinely impressed while also a little unsettled. "Will trumps skill. Nice one, Dad."

"Oh, kid, you wouldn't believe how many of those I've got in my quiver. And, you come along with me and wait till you see how quickly your quiver gets filled. I'll have you a quivering mess."

Entrees arrive. Venison-mushroom risotto for me, veal chops for him.

"Am I selling? Am I selling?" he asks anxiously.

"Ah, Dad . . . ," I say, and hope that says enough.

"You'll think about it," he says.

My venison is so vital, I feel it breathing inside me. I feel stronger already.

"I don't think I will," I say.

He visibly deflates, chews his veal more slowly. He adores veal, and I hate disappointing him.

"You could just try it, for a while."

"What if I wanted to go to school?" I don't—at least not as I sit here, I don't. And he knows it because he knows me.

"I will *take* you to school, boy," he says, poking a sharp knife in my direction. "Come on. I will be your school."

"Dad?"

"Fine. Then if you want to go to that other kind, with the students and the football games and the drug orgies, it'll still be there for you."

I just don't know. I don't know anything.

That's not true. I know something.

It's all about her.

That's what I know. And it's crippling me.

"Get me another beer, and I'll think about thinking about it."

"Okay," he says, grinning and waving at the waiter. "But I have to warn you, I have an employment contract here in my briefcase, and it won't matter whether you recall signing it or not."

He does make me laugh. I do like his company. That is, spending time with him, as opposed to his business operation. There could probably be worse things.

"So," he says as the pint lands on the table between us, glistening beads of condensation slaloming down its sides, "what do you know about this lottery ticket thing?"

I sigh. I am already sick of this subject.

"Well, from what I understand, one buys a ticket, picks some numbers, and then has about a one in triple-infinity chance of winning more money than one spent on the ticket."

"Ha. Good one, O. But I think you know that I am referring to the rumors."

"That One Who Knows has miraculously won the thing for a second time?"

"Well . . . no. That your girlfriend has actually won."

"Are you going to finish that?" I say, reaching right over and spearing a veal chop that I bring to my plate. Passive aggression at its most tasty.

"Oh, by all means," he says. "As for your girlfriend?"

"I don't have a girlfriend, and I believe you know that."

"Sorry, Son. But did she? Win? Does she have the ticket in her possession?"

I scoop a big spoonful of risotto and plunk it down onto his plate. I take a long pull on the beer. I take a bite of the veal chop.

"Is this you changing the subject?" he asks.

I take the lump of risotto back and pop it into my mouth. I return the empty chop bone to his plate.

"It was just a question, Oliver."

"It's none of my business, Dad. I hope she did win and that she's going to be the happy heartbreaker for the rest of her life, but she didn't win, and she's working every possible shift at that stupid shop and she's walking dogs to the moon and back, and I hope that *that* makes her the happiest heart-breaker in the solar system, but frankly I have *no* insight into this situation, nor into any other situation that involves Junie Blue, other than that *every* situation involves Junie Blue and every situation involving Junie Blue is making *me* blue."

I take another gulp of the beer and peer over the rim of the glass at my chastened-looking father sipping his water through a straw.

"You're upset," he says wisely.

We stare across at each other for several seconds, both drink glasses remaining like shields in front of our faces.

And I laugh. "Yeah, Dad. I guess I am."

"Love is like getting fat, O. If you take a long time building it up, it takes a long time burning it off."

I shake my head at the depth of his wisdom. "It's like *fat*?"

He laughs. "Yeah, that might not be my best work there."

"You ever been fat, Dad?"

"Oh, God, no."

"So, then, how—"

"Unless you're still going with the metaphor. Simile? Whatever. If fat means love here, then, oh, God, yes. I am fat inside out for your mother. Make no mistake, Son. I am a blob for your mother."

"Wow. What can I say? That's just sweet as hell. And no, I don't think I want any dessert, thanks."

"Ah," he says, calling for the check. In seconds he is paying and signing, and as I finish the scraps and dregs, he fills the conversational void. "So, you don't believe she's got the ticket?" he says casually.

"Thanks for lunch," I say, and beat it out of there before he has even calculated the tip. He's shockingly slow with numbers.

Six

I have just about convinced myself that I can move on. By "move on" I mean I can have thoughts that don't entirely revolve around Junie. I can consider my father's offer of a job for life—no—and the prospect of college—not yet—and what that leaves me for near-term options—beats the squat out of me—without my mind being paralytic with concerns and worries and speculations about the existence of lovely June.

And then my phone does that thing that it does. Message.

I'm coming over.

It's from her.

And just like that, as if all the psychological masonry that I had just carefully tapped and pointed into place has been rocked with a 6.5 tremor, I come spectacularly to rubble again.

I jump out of bed, grab some clean underwear—that's right, this time I was doing *exactly* the type of mind-clearing exercise they think I'm always doing—and I get dressed as if I am going to Wimbledon or boating or my own baptism, but in my bright beautiful whites I am confident that this is the sunny reboot of my summer right here.

The doorbell rings, and I hear my mother padding to the door—but sorry, Mom, I cannot be denied—and I take three stairs at a go and practically break my ankle at the bottom, but I wobble and career to the door first and fling it open on the wrong, wrong, wrong shade of goddamn blackened Blue.

"What are you doing here, Ronny?" I say.

"Is that what passes for hospitality in this house?" he says.

"Yes," I snarl.

"No," Mom says, extending her hand to shake the beast's big meaty paw.

"You have lovely hands," he says, and he *kisses* one of them. A noise comes straight through my stomach wall, like when you need to retch but you fight it down. I won't fight next time. "Lovely artist's hands."

"Is there something I can do for you, Mr. Blue," she over-polites.

"Mr. Blue is a weenie Bobby Vinton song from the 1970s. I'm Ronny. Especially to a lovely lady such as yourself."

She's courteous, but she's not a dope. "Yes, thank you. So, what brings you here?"

"An appointment," he says.

"What are you talking about?" I say. "And what are you doing with Junie's phone again?"

"You're an inquisitive little chap today. As it happens, Miss June—hey, sounds like she's naked in a magazine, don't it? Anyway, she happened to leave her phone behind again."

"Where is she?"

"Another holiday, I guess."

"So," Mom interjects.

"So," he answers, "I pick up this business card, right. Your business card," he says, pulling my mother's card out of his breast pocket. "And it says right there on the back that there's a sitting scheduled here this morning. And I remember, I was supposed to be having a sitting, so apparently it's been scheduled for me. So, apparently, I better get myself over here. Can't be upsetting the artiste, you know what I mean?"

"Where is Leona?" Mom says in a cool way that bears no resemblance to any version of her warm self I have ever heard.

"Home," he says, all happy-smiley. "Where she's supposed to be. Why do you ask?"

There is a crackling hot silence.

"Shall we get to it, then?" he says, that infuriatingly happy mug. He's chewing all the scenery around, like an actor hamming it up for the cameras.

Mom sits in her usual artist seat with a grim determination I usually only associate with the day she does her taxes. The portrait's subject, on the other hand, looks like he's settling into one of the better rides at Disneyland.

"This is really a lovely place you have here," Ronny says, taking everything in, the way I imagine a burglar would.

"Please face front," Mom says sternly.

"Where's June?" I say, standing over him. This must look like an interrogation from an old war movie.

"I told you," he says.

"No, you didn't."

"You know, you don't have to be here, O," Mom says.

"I don't mind," I say.

"What do you think about that lottery business, nobody coming forth to claim it?" Ronny says. Hard to tell who he's talking to.

"Interesting," Mom says.

"Interesting, yes," he says.

Knowing this particular choreography, I jump ahead. "Why don't you ask her yourself?"

"Think I didn't try that already?"

"So, what did she say?"

He pauses. "I can't repeat it in front of your mother."

"Ha," Mom says, a welcome spasm of joy in the middle of her determined sketching.

"Good for Junie," I say.

"Shouldn't you be out playin' tennis?" he snaps. "Or croquet? That's the kind of thing your people play, isn't it? Croquet?"

"No."

"Then why are you dressed like that?"

I look down at my bright and clean and sporty getup, which feels so embarrassingly inappropriate now and was probably embarrassingly inappropriate before—Junie would have mocked me more than anyone—and I am thrown back to my childish high hopes of earlier. I feel stupid, and bereft.

"You look lovely," Mom says, making things infinitely worse.

I leave and go to my room, where I change into some jeans that are too heavy for the heat and a black button-down shirt that is the wrong color but the right material—linen— so I can look my version of tough while still surviving in breathable fabrics.

When I return to the scene of the art crime, Mom is already wrapping up the session. It lasted maybe one third of the time that Leona's did, and who wouldn't want to spend precious life minutes with the one rather than the other.

Ronny hops to his feet, anxious to see, certain of the drawing's greatness already.

Mom quickly throws a smock over it.

"Oh, you can't see this version of the work, Ronny. It's far too preliminary."

"You need me to come back for another—"

"Not at all," she blurts, practically lunging to stuff the

words back into his mouth. "I have all I need to work with. Now it's time for me to live with it for a spell."

I get a chill thinking about my poor, decent-hearted mother living with *it* for even a while.

"Oh," he says. "Okay, then. You're the artist. So lemme just . . ." He reaches into the baggy pocket of his baggy shiny black pants and pulls out a folded hunk of currency, a thicket of bills that looks like a fat green cross section of a calzone.

"Oh, oh," she says, holding both hands outstretched defensively, blocking her very sight of the dough as if the guy were waving his manliness around, which, of course, he is. "We'll, ah . . . we'll wait and see how it comes out before we talk about anything like that. We'll let you know when it's ready. Right, O?"

"We'll be in touch," I say, flat.

I see him to the door as Mom remains rooted to her place, and her art.

"Thanks for having me," he hisses. "Fun to be inside your world. See how your type lives. Just like I imagined. What does your old man do again?"

"I want to see her," I say, this coming from I don't know where.

"You, *want* . . . ? Listen to me, sonny. You keep talking to me like that, and you'll be happy enough to see *tomorrow*, you understand?"

I understand, of course. We have reached that unfortunate place where Ronny Blue and I understand each other
quite clearly.

Not a place I've ever wanted to be.

I slam the door.

The horseflies are savaging me. Monstrous little things. They
mostly leave you alone, until you go into the water and come
back out. Salt water is like some combination of Worcester-
shire sauce and meat tenderizer to them, and it's chow time
once you settle onto the sand again.

So I don't settle. I bodysurf, bodysurf some more. Come
out, get punctured a few more times, go back and bodysurf
some more. It is my kind of beach day, hot but overcast,
sparsely populated, nice surf for the body.

It is the finest and purest of all water sports. I feel like
I harness the force of the whole damn ocean when I flat-
ten and fly the top of a wave all the way into the sand. If
you glide rather than jump into it, if you catch the exact
break point, if you just make yourself available, place yourself
on top of the wave, then the wave accepts you, and there is
no better feeling I have ever found, no closer you'll ever get
to being properly owned by the sea. And what higher state
could there be than that?

Board surfing is okay. But there's a board. A level of remove.

Your belly can't scrape along the sandy bottom with a board.

"Are you following me or something?" I say as I lie right there where the latest white horse has deposited me.

"What, the beach belongs to you now?" Malcolm says, walking in up to his ankles. "I know your dad's a master of the universe these days, but—"

"My father is hardly a master of the universe. Where do you get this stuff?"

"Ear to the ground, my man. I've got my ear to the ground, and so nothing eludes me. You should try it."

I turn my head and drop my ear flat to the sand. The remains of a wave come in and go up my nose.

"Goof," he says, wading out into the water. I get up and join him.

He catches a wave right away, surfs it competently but jumps too hard into it and rides too low to go all the way in. I am childishly pleased at his mediocrity, and it is possible this is written on my face as he returns.

"Who cares," he says. "It's not like it's tennis or anything."

"You going to play at college?" I ask.

"I hope to. If you come along, I bet we could make it in doubles."

"Hnn," I say, September considerations chasing me right back into now. "Junie is gone on another *holiday*," I say, and I can hear the sombre in my own voice.

"Yeah," he says, sizing up another wave. "Don't worry about it, though. She'll be fine."

He takes off, a little higher and lighter this time, and I follow his path all the way in. Then I follow him. I'm not surfing, though. I'm stomping.

"What do you mean by that?" I demand. "What do you know about it?"

He is wallowing in the shallows, about ten inches of water. He shushes around, eel-like, flips over onto his back to see me seeing him.

"Nothing. Junie is one tough chicklet, that's all. She can handle anything."

"What's she handling, Mal?"

He grows quickly, visibly uneasy. Flips back over and starts lobster-walking away from me into the deeper water.

"Nothing. How would I know. Jesus, paranoid."

I don't know where this next thing comes from. It sure doesn't come from my history or my nature or anywhere I recognize in myself.

I launch myself and dive right onto Malcolm's back. When I am there, I get a grip on his neck, and I force his head all the way under the water. I feel his face thump into the sand, and I've got him in such an awkward position that it's almost too easy to do this. I grind his face into the ocean floor as he flails back at me over his shoulders.

"Tell me what is happening," I growl at him, insanely, since he cannot possibly meet my request. "Tell me, Ronny Blue ball boy, what is happening to Junie, or I'll kill you, I swear."

I have him under for six, eight, ten seconds, my knees now digging hard into his back, when I sense he is weakening. And I sense . . . myself.

I throw myself sideways off him and kneel there in the water as Malcolm surges up desperately and does an hour's worth of deep breathing in ten seconds to regain the amount of his life I choked away.

"Are you *demented*?" he gasps, first kneeling, then on all fours. "You . . . have got something majorly wrong with you, O."

I almost say I'm sorry. I come close. But not that close.

"Where is she?" I say calmishly.

"Kiss my ass."

"I won't. Might kick it, though."

"Eat me."

He stands up, wobbles a bit, then makes his way toward the beach.

"If anything bad happens to her," I call at his back, still on my knees as the waves bump and nudge at me.

He stops to address me directly.

"Know what? Trifling with you is one thing. Junie could

mess with you forever and never get burnt. But that chick's had a lesson in humility coming to her for a long time, and I hope now she gets it."

I jump up out of the water. He turns and bolts.

I stand there watching him run and letting the horseflies stab at me mercilessly.

"Are you serious?" I say to Mom.

"You know I treat art with the utmost seriousness and respect," she says.

We are standing in front of the pair of portraits she has done, of Mr. and Mrs. Blue, and I do not believe I have ever been prouder of my gentle mental mother.

"You captured them both, so uncannily, spookily well." I know she feels likewise because she has even framed them.

"Well," she says theatrically, "that is what I do."

"I thought you said, though, that you needed another sitting with Leona?"

"I didn't *need* one. I just wanted one. *She* needed it. But when her rutting rhinoceros of a husband stole her date, I thought it best just to finish up. We'll get together some other way."

"Well, damn, you got her. She's luminous."

"Thank you, Son. That means a lot to me."

We continue to consider the works before us, silently

studying like real art gallery patrons. Then I start laughing, rumbling, cackling.

"He is going to be so furious."

She allows herself a small giggle, then goes all professional once more.

"Thank you, Son. That means a lot to me."

I phone Maxine, possibly to inform her that the portraits are ready.

"Is she there?" I ask.

"Yeah, O, she is."

I hear loud voices in the background. In that household this does not have tremendous meaning.

"I'll come over. To deliver the pictures."

"Maybe not," she says over increasing volume.

"I'll be right there."

"No—," she says as I hang up.

"Mom," I say, "can I deliver the portraits for you?"

"What, are you going to lug them over under each arm? Those are good, solid oak frames."

"How delicate do you think I am, Mother?"

"Oh, I'm not worried about you. It's my good work I'm trying to protect."

"Guess you'd better lend me your car, then, huh?"

"Guess I'd better, then."

• • •

I can hear them even before I turn off the car's engine. I park at the curb right in front of the house, then quick-step up the walk.

I knock once, and Maxie throws open the door.

"I thought I told you . . . ," she says, only half-angry. She walks into the house, and I follow.

Junie's parents are shouting at each other across the breakfast bar in the kitchen, and I don't care. I look around not-so-subtly until Maxie points me up the stairs. I still have the pictures under my arms as I take the stairs two at a time and knock on Junie's door with my forehead.

"If you're female, come in," she says.

I lean one of the pictures on the floor against the door-frame and open the door.

As soon as I see her, my heart fills, my eyes fill.

She is sitting like a schoolkid on the side of her bed, back straight, hands folded in her lap as she stares at the floor. I see her in profile. Then slowly she turns to face me.

Her Creamsicle pillow of a top lip is clearly swollen. There is a bruise on her forearm that looks like she's been hit with a baseball.

"Ah, Junie," I say.

"Ah, O," she says.

I put the pictures against the wall, close the door, and

inch my way over to the bed. I kneel down on the floor and fold my hands over her folded hands.

"I boldly came in, even though I'm not a female."

"Yeah," she says, puffing out a pained little smile, "but you're pretty close."

I feign shock and hurt, because I am not man enough to manage the real thing.

"Hey, I nearly killed a guy over you, I'll have you know."

The statement is too far outside normal reality for her to consider. "Thanks," she says.

The hollering continues downstairs. I hear Ronny shout, "You know how she's making me look? Huh?"

"I may have to do it again," I say, tipping my head in the direction of the racket and the racketeer.

"He's concerned about the way he *looks*," she says, shaking her head. "Is that the biggest joke you ever heard, or what?"

"It's a pretty big joke," I say. "I'll laugh later, though."

I am still kneeling at her feet, holding on to her, and desperately searching my brain and my experience for a clue as to what comes next. I've got nothing, so it's down to guess-work.

"You got stuff you want to tell me?" I ask.

"I do not," she says.

"You got stuff you do not want to tell me but should tell me anyway?"

"I do not."

I nod and stare a little more, which I could do all night if she wouldn't eventually kick me out.

"Well, this is progressing well," I say. "How 'bout I get the ball rolling, then. Um, did you win the lottery, Sweet Junie Blue Lies?"

"No, I did not, Lyin' O'Brien."

"Well, then. It sure would be helpful if whoever did win it came forward and claimed, huh?"

"Yeah. S'pose it would."

"Then they could take up the amazing offer and proceed to lead a charmed life, while the rest of us could calm down."

That balloon just floats there, in the limited space between us.

"I *say*," I say, "then they could take up—"

"Charmed," she says, floaty, an incantation.

Ronny is clearly now bellowing up from the foot of the stairs. "There are rules. You don't have to love the rules, but you do have to play by them. It's about the principles."

"*Principles*," Junie repeats, with a bolted-on grin that looks chillingly like a doctor's dummy skull. "If he gets any funnier, I might have to start applauding."

I cannot help staring at her. I probably did that too much in the past, and that didn't help my case too much. But I couldn't help it then and I cannot help it now, even if the staring is more specific and concerned now.

I reach up and touch her face, cupping her chin in my hand and lightly brushing the swelled lip with my thumb.

"Is that him doing this? Ronny?"

She pushes my hand away. "Well, since there is no *this*, I guess the answer is no. Or yes, since there is no *this*, so both answers are equally true."

"Or equally lies," I say.

She stands up, leaving me genuflecting to her absence as she paces angrily. "Don't talk about me like I'm some kind of victim, O, 'cause I'm not, okay?"

"Okay, okay, of course you're not. It's just—"

"Just nothing. Don't even try, right?"

"You could use some help, though, surely."

"Surely not."

"Come *on*, Junie. You need help."

"I do not *need* anything, thank you."

"Yes, you do." This may be the first time I have ever attempted to speak sternly to her. "You don't want to admit it, but you need me. Jesus, your pigheadedness."

She stops pacing and turns on me, and her body language alone is enough to discourage me from ever attempting the stern-speak again. She has both index fingers in front of her— in between us—pointing toward the ceiling as she bites off each word with ruthless precision. "I do not need you, sweetheart. That's for damn sure. I have been fine and will be fine without you or anyone else. Hear me clearly on this, Oliver, and world: I am nobody's bitch. Nobody's."

I feel the weight of her words, of her feelings, practically increasing the force of gravity itself. It's probably a good thing that I am already on my knees, in supplicant pose.

"Sorry, June," I say. "I know all that already."

"You should," she snaps.

"I do," I say.

"Well, you should," she says, reviving a familiar old debating style that got us nowhere on several occasions. But for the circumstances, I could really enjoy that right now.

For whatever reason Ronny is raging with increased vigor downstairs.

"Where does this wind up?" I ask her.

She shrugs. "He could have a stroke. Which would be nice."

"Yeah, that would be nice."

There is a knock on the door.

"Password?" Junie says.

"Ronny sucks the big one," Maxine says solemnly.

"You may enter," Junie says.

"This has been quite a while," Max says, closing the door behind her. "You guys getting busy up here? Even with all that racket? I'd never be able to concentrate, myself."

"How's it going down there?" I ask as jovially as the situation will allow.

"I should ask you the same thing," she says, noting that I have not managed to get up out of my kneeling pose. "You getting kinky, or are you doing that confession thing you people are so keen on?"

I stand to attention.

"Honestly, Maxie," Junie says, gesturing toward the door, the stairs, and the jackass.

"I know, I know," she says. "But first, sorry, I am required to ask you . . ." She drops into a robotic voice. "June Blue, have you won the lottery, by any chance?"

"No, ma'am," Junie answers in the same voice.

"Righteo," she says. "Now that that's out of the way, I should tell you he's into the tequila."

"Aw, hell," Junie says.

"Hell. Exactly," Maxie says. "I estimate that we are now at approximately hell minus eighteen minutes."

Junie sighs and walks around to the other side of her bed, looks like she is going to sit or lie down, then changes her mind, walks back to her sister, back to her bed.

This is a vision I never expected to see. It is a vision nobody should ever see; Junie Blue lost. She is right now unsure and unsettled, and it is so unnatural to her and just plain wrong that I am physically queasy just being present for it.

"That does it," I say. "I'm going to go talk to him."

Both of the women rush to get between me and the door, both protesting the unwisdom of that idea. They seem genuinely worried for me, though Maxine is simultaneously spluttering laughter at my folly.

"I think you should get out," Max says to her sister.

"Well, that's my plan, Maxie, and you know that. I'm moving just as soon as I—"

"I don't mean that. I mean, like, now. Clear out so that his little mind will lack a focal point for his meanness. Nothing good can come from you being here tonight."

"Excellent idea," I say. "Superb idea, Maxie. We'll go to my house. It'll be great. My mom will—"

Junie is shaking her head.

"Junie," I plead, "why not?"

"Yeah," Maxine says, "why not? I've been there, and that place is wonderful. What's not to like? Beats this dump every which way."

Junie just continues to shake her head, and I don't need to ask her again, because we both already know how she feels about it. She rarely ever came to my house. Said the place made her uneasy. The house did, the roses did, the neighborhood did, the smell did. My parents did, even though she said she liked them fine and my father was charmed to near baby talk by her, and my mother clearly sensed the situation and worked up a sweat trying to put her at ease. Junie went so far as to say one time that the house gave her the creeps.

"What if we go someplace else, then?" I say.

She eyes me suspiciously. She is hanging in there, but it is clear that events have been taking their toll, and she is looking weary. The sound of a glass shattering in the kitchen adds a little fillip of specialness.

"Where?" she says.

"Not sure, exactly," I say, though I am a little sure. My insides have shifted into an entirely different realm as I contemplate the romance of running away.

And I do realize that if Junie could hear my thoughts, I would not have gotten past the word "romance" without a clap across the ear. Still, I persevere.

"Just a place, a hotel, like, to get away for a night. Or maybe two—"

"Ah, *two*?" she says.

"Go, O!" Maxie cheers.

"Quiet, you," Junie says.

"Fine, but I won't be quiet for long, because this sounds like a superb offer you're getting. And if you're silly enough to pass . . . Well, let me just say that *one* of us will be keeping this lovely gentleman company."

My body shoots through, toes to top hat, with adrenaline or testosterone, or whatever combination my inner chemist has just produced, but my foolish head is spinning with that talk, and the rest of my parts are about to join it.

But that's not even the best part. The best part is Junie Blue's reaction to the provocation.

She looks at her sister with eyes narrowed and sideways. Her nostrils flare. Her lips pull in, tight and hard.

That bothered her.

And I am delighted beyond words at this. It is a mighty effort to fight down a gigantic smile, until she finally says the two most romantic words, "I suppose," and I need to fight no more.

She throws a few things into a bag, and Maxine goes over to where the framed portraits are leaning, wrapped in their brown-paper protection.

"And you guys can slip out while I create the perfect diversion with the presentation of the birthday gifts."

"When is his birthday?" I ask.

"Today," she says matter-of-factly as she tears the wrapping off one.

"Really? No offense, but it doesn't appear very birthday-like," I say.

"Hey," Max laughs. "I *said* there was tequila."

Then her laughter abruptly stops. With Junie standing behind her now, she takes in the vision of their mother, in the vision of my mother.

"My God," Maxie says.

"O," Junie says, covering her mouth with her hand and talking through it. "That's exquisite. I mean . . ."

"That's Leona," Max says. "That is *her*. That is every bit of her."

"Your mother is a genius," Junie says.

"According to my mom, Leona did all the work," I say.

Maxine then turns to the companion portrait, tears the wrapping off.

There is a pause of maybe four seconds. Then critical appraisal.

"Bwaaa-haa-haa-haa." Maxine is genuinely, heartily convulsed with laughter. "Perfect," she gasps. "My God, you can practically smell the sulfur coming off him."

Junie is squeezing my arm now. She is not laughing as uproariously as her sister is, but there is a deeply satisfied gigantic grin lighting her up. "I'll say it again, your mom is a genius."

"Hurry up now," Max says, gathering up the portraits. "I can't wait a minute longer to unveil these."

"Yeah," Junie says, "and I seriously believe we will want to be gone when that moment arrives."

The three of us slip down the stairs quietly. Then Junie and I split off for the front door while Max, giggling, heads for the sounds of cracking ice and growling in the kitchen.

"Heeyy, birthday boy," I hear her say just as we close the door, and I marvel at her fearlessness.

We get out to the car, and I start it up and put it in gear. Junie has just rolled down her window to let in the warm evening air and freedom she is clearly experiencing for this moment.

Then suddenly a smash, and we see a chunky oak frame come flying out the front window, bouncing to a rest flat on the lawn.

We share a loud, nervous but hearty laugh as we peel out to the sound of Ronny's incredulous, "What the hell is this? Huh? Funny? This is funny, maybe?"

He appears to be addressing the portrait itself, through the shattered window, demanding that it respond.

Seven

My selfish and immature mind has managed to transcend all of the unpleasant realities of the current state of things, to the point where I am nearly euphoric as I navigate my mother's car through the local streets, out to the parkway, and head into the city. I am thrilled to be in Junie's company for an extended period of time. I am thrilled to be tooling around on an ideal summer night with a lovely girl in the passenger seat for all the world to see, even if it appears nobody but me is seeing it.

And, God help me, I am thrilled to be playing the part of the shining knight I have been so aching to be for her.

Let's hear it for selfish immaturity.

Junie has relaxed to the point of semiconsciousness, as the breeze does mad whippy things to her hair and the singer on the radio encourages us to meet him tonight in Atlantic City. I could. I could just about continue on, to Atlantic City or wherever else Junie and I could find the adventure of our lives.

Another day, maybe.

"Where are we?" she asks without opening her eyes.

"We're here."

"We're here?" she asks, a playful smile coming across her lips while her eyes remain closed. "But we were already at *here*. We're always *here*. I thought we were supposed to be headed for *there*?"

I lean over and say right into her ear. "We are headed there. We're headed here, there, and everywhere, don't you worry. But right now I need to head inside and see if they have got a room for us. Want to wait while I check?"

"Yes," she says.

I breathe in a little more of her before I exit the vehicle and enter the hotel.

The hotel, one of the newer ones in the old city, sits in a spectacular spot between the redeveloped waterfront and the financial district. Every room has views over either the harbor or the heart of the city. It's half a block from my dad's office, which is how I learned about the place. He's been to a number of fancy functions here, and always comes home raving about every detail. On a few occasions Dad's company has sprung for a little holiday here for a business associate who Dad considers a VIP, and whose money he would like to get his hands on.

"If you ever want to impress a girl, Son, this is the place for it," he has said more than once.

Well, I really want to impress a girl.

Although there is an element of risk involved, as this brings into play a contentious issue between the very girl and myself.

"Of course, Mr. O'Brien. We have a room available," the very nice French man at the front desk says when I produce the credit card that looks like it is made of semiprecious metal. Okay, precious.

Junie loathes this card.

It is, of course, sponsored by my father. It will continue to be sponsored by my father until summer's end, at which time I will be required to make a decision of some kind, either winding up in school or working and paying my own bills. The truth is, I don't even know what the card's limit is, if it even has one, but everyone knows I would not be the type to take advantage of the arrangement. I have made every attempt to keep the thing tucked securely in its wallet parking space. In fact, even though I used it only rarely, as a high school credit card it would be fair to say it was overkill.

Which is just what Junie would have liked to do to it.

This, surely, would have to qualify as a reasonable exception.

"Would you prefer a city-side or harbor-view room?" the nice gentleman asks.

I am about to answer when a mini-paralysis hits. I don't

want to get even the slightest thing wrong here, and I could
see Junie picking either one. Only, if I pick one, her pick
would without a doubt wind up being the other.

"Can you hold on just a second?"

"Certainly," he says.

I quick-step across the lobby, then run the rest of the way
to where the car is parked at a metered, unpaid spot. Junie is
sound asleep until I tap on the window. Slowly she comes to,
rubbing her eyes, looking around confusedly. Then she seems
to have some recollection of who I am, and rolls down the
window.

"If you had your choice . . . which you do . . . would you
prefer a city-side view or a harbor-side view?"

Clarity is coming to her quickly now, possibly too
quickly. She starts looking past me, behind me, then up. And
up, and up.

"That?" she says, pointing at the glistening glass of the
hotel.

"Yeah," I say.

She rolls up the window again. "I'm gonna sleep in the
car."

She closes her eyes, and I start rapping on the window.
"What?" she says after she's opened the window again.

"Come on. They have a nice room for us, and—"

"Oh, O, I couldn't. I just . . . Oh, I couldn't." She is

looking up at the beautiful building as if it were Godzilla thundering toward us.

I reach into the car and take her hand. I try to make my begging as dignified as possible, but if that doesn't work, I am more than prepared to go the other way with it.

"Please, Junie? Listen, I know how you feel, and I respect that. You don't like flash, and you don't like fancy, and you don't like fuss. . . ." My voice trails off, and I am left hanging there wondering if I ever had a finish to that thought prepared in the first place.

She waits. "Yeah, and so . . ."

"And so . . ." I feel like I'm just going to burst, and God knows what will come out of me then, so in a panic I try to supply words instead. "And so . . . I want you just this once to let me make a fancy flash fuss over you, Junie Blue. That's it. That's the truth, and beyond that, I got nothing. So please, please let me just do that?"

She looks up at the imposing building again, down at me, up at the building.

"I don't know about this, O, I really don't."

Finally inspiration comes riding in.

"What would Ronny think?"

She splutters an immediate and messy laugh. "You kiddin' me? He'd pee himself with envy and spite and—"

I lean way in toward her, hoping to achieve a winning

combination of conspiratorially and intimately breathy. "Happy birthday, Ronny."

It may not be that my gambit was all that clever, and it may be that the prospect of more pleading was too much to bear, or maybe she just finally needed a bed, but when I open the door gallantly for her, she graciously steps out.

I try to take her bag, but she pulls it roughly away. "Don't get carried away now, Lancelot."

Yeah," I say, very excited, trying not to seem very excited. "Sorry. What was I thinking, huh?"

"Harbor-side," she says as we walk up to the entrance.

"Great," I say.

The doorman opens the door for us, and I feel Junie be uncharacteristically reticent, ever-so-lightly sort of clinging to me, two bunches of my shirt in her fists.

"If you'd like to give me the keys, Mr. O'Brien, I'll be glad to have your car parked in our garage."

Okay, now even I am a little jolted. We're not even checked in, and it's like I'm a regular.

"Well," I say, "sure. Great, thanks." I slap the keys and a bill into his palm, and he thanks me kindly, ushers us through, and says, "Have a pleasant stay, Mr. O'Brien." Then the kicker. "Mrs. O'Brien," he adds with a gallant small bow.

Halfway between the door and the desk Junie asks, "They *know* you? How the hell do they know you?"

I do not mean to lie, but how can you not enjoy the moment when the moment may well be the finest one of your life? "Oh, didn't you know about me? Oh, babe, I get this *everywhere*. There's plenty more where that came from, trust me."

Still hanging on to my shirt, she whispers hard into my ear, "There better not be."

"Ah, Mr. O'Brien," the reception man says. I start to turn my head to make more of that moment, but she gives me that pinch in the back, the little nip with just the fingernails that has the force of twenty horseflies.

"Ah-hah," I say involuntarily.

"I see you have brought in the consultant on the city-side–harbor-side question. Excellent. And the verdict is . . ."

"Harbor-side, my good man."

"Room 1424," he says, sliding across a form for my signature, along with two key cards and my credit card.

"Oh, that thing," Junie whispers coldly as I sign and take the stuff away.

"You were prepared for our decision," I say to the man, impressed.

"Oh, yes, sir. I knew you'd be harbor-side before you were halfway across the lobby. Have a very pleasant stay, folks."

"Thank you very much," I say, and as I turn from the desk toward the bank of elevators, I work my right hand up my back and just manage to reach one of Junie's fists. I forcibly convince that fist to engage with my hand rather than my shirt, and I am feeling pretty good as we get onto the elevator hand in hand. The mirrored back wall of the elevator confirms my good feeling.

"Now will you try to relax a bit, Mrs. O'Brien?"

"Fourteen floors is a long way down, Mr. O'Brien," she says, but I'm pretty sure she doesn't mean it. In fact, I'm pretty sure I feel her squeeze my hand a little harder.

We get off, follow the signage to 1424, and it is with great anticipation that I am poised with the key card to open the door.

"O," she says, tugging me slightly back from the door.

"What's up, Junie?"

She is looking down at her feet, then up at the high ceiling and each way down the endless corridor.

"Don't laugh at me."

I cannot even imagine where that thought came from. But it is the easiest response I've had to formulate today.

"Don't be absurd," I say, perhaps running a bit low on romantic language, but my delivery, I am sure, said what I meant.

"I've never stayed in a hotel before in my life," she says.

It's the kind of thing you don't think about. Or at least I don't. Not that I've been in a million hotels myself, but I've been in a few—on family holidays, a couple of short business trips with Dad a long time ago. But it just seems kind of auto-matic, to think of this experience as part of everybody's expe-rience, to think of it as not that big a deal, and it makes Junie, for these few seconds, feel just that little bit foreign to me.

And she clearly thinks of this as a big-deal issue.

"Okay, so what?" I say to her as she actually takes another step back from our hotel room door, and I fear a terrible regression.

"I feel so stupid," she says.

"No," I plead, rushing to fill the space between us. "No, no, no, no, Junie. My God, no."

I attempt to give her a comforting hug, but with her bag hanging off her shoulder and her arms folded mightily in front of her, it's like comforting a little vending machine.

"I feel so wrong here, O."

"Trust me. Would you trust me? It's nothing special. Once we get inside, that's just, y'know, our room. No big deal. Right?"

The vending machine reluctantly and quietly says, "Right."

In an effort to build on that momentum, I turn and rush to the door, pulling Junie behind me by her belt, inserting the key card into the lock with the other hand. The lock pops, I push open the door, and we are in. I usher Junie farther into the room, then hurry to close the door behind us.

"Oh, for Christsake," Junie snaps.

I step up behind her and take in what she's taking in. The room.

"Oh," I say. "Oh. Well, um. Oh."

"For Christsake," she says.

"Listen, just don't look at it. You're very tired, so maybe you should just, maybe, just go straight to bed. . . ."

She turns, toward the bed.

"Oh, for Christsake."

It's a pretty nice bed. The duvet is as thick as my mattress at home. I estimate it's a king-and-a-half size. The layout of the *room* they have given us is quite something. That huge bed is the centerpiece, with the footboard facing the massive curtained window on one side. Above and beyond the headboard are what look like a pair of Japanese-style sliding windows with semi-opaque greenish sea-glass-looking panels in them. The windows reach from the top of the headboard almost up to the ceiling. Soft light glows from the other side of the panels, a light that is clearly telling Junie Blue to come to it. She drops her bag, jumps up, and walks across the bed to those sliders like an old movie detective who says, *All right. I know you're in there.*

"Oh, for—"

That would be the bathroom. She stands there up on the bed, the bedroom now open to the gleaming huge bathroom, the whole place open, really from the shower stall right on through to the window wall. If one sat on that Japanese windowsill—and one has every intention of doing just that before we leave here—you could look down on one side right onto the bed, and down on the other side, right onto the bathtub. You could also see just about every other corner of the place from that perch, not to mention the views out across the harbor beyond, but probably that bed-bath axis would be enough to keep me occupied.

She stares at me, all bug-eyed and accusatory.

"The room has nice flow, huh?" is my surrender line.

But she's not through. She marches the quarter mile from the pillows to the foot of the bed, hops right down, and makes a dash for the curtains before I can even slow her down. She whips the curtain back—runs it all the way, actually, from left to right until all is revealed.

And all is quite something. My parents gave me a helicopter trip over the city as part of my thirteenth birthday, and I don't recall the view of the harbor being as good as this one. And the night is clear and perfect, illuminating all the boats. It's almost making me mad, now, how relentless this fabulosity is.

"What did they do, bring in extra friggin' sparkly boats and stars just for us?" I say.

She is staring now, speechless. I stand right behind her,

with about six inches of buffer air between us, as I do not dare to make contact.

I know that at any other time, under any other circumstances, I would see the same magnificence here that most people see.

Right now it feels perverse.

"I know," I say somberly. "For Christsake."

She pauses a couple of seconds.

"Let's go see the bathroom," she says.

This is when she drowns me, I imagine.

I wouldn't even know how to define the opulence of the bathroom. Everything is a kind of pale rose marble. There are four complete neighborhoods in here for various functions. She tugs me over to the enormous tub, with its rack of beauty products. "What does a person even *do* with six different controls on a bathtub? Does it fly? Can we take it for a spin around the harbor tomorrow?"

I think that is funny, but I am too apprehensive to laugh.

Until she does. As she takes a second, then a third lap of the bathroom, Junie begins laughing a most incredulous, disarming, confused, helpless laugh. She makes emphatic, wordless gestures toward this shiny item and that, and finally just holds both hands straight up in the air.

"You see," I say, standing my ground at a distance and pointing at her, "that could be seen as either the international gesture of surrender, or touchdown, so I'm not sure . . . Oh, wait. Now that I think of it, those are both good things."

She grabs me by both hands, pulls me over to the sink, and then spins me around to look out, through the opening in the sliding windows.

From this spot you can see everything, the dazzling bathroom, then out over the big bed, to the glass-topped sideboard on the right-hand wall with the massive TV, and straight ahead to the glass wall, out to the harbor and the stars and stars above and beyond the sea.

I turn my back on all that, to look into the face of Junie Blue. It's a fine trade.

"So, now you feel like you belong here?" I ask hopefully, stupidly falling into a hug with her.

"Oh, absolutely not," she says, surprisingly chipper. "But I am taking small comfort in the knowledge that *nobody* belongs here. I'm embracing the absurdity."

"Yes," I say, hugging her tighter. "That really just encapsulates pretty much everything I have ever asked you to do. Yes! Embrace the absurdity, Junie Blue!"

She puts a finger to my lips. "Shhh. For the moment. I am *temporarily* prepared to embrace the absurdity. But this is not real."

"Great," I say. "Understood."

"So . . . ," she says, gazing over my shoulder, "how much did this cost?"

"Shhh," I say, my finger to her lips. A shock of something nasty bolts through my body as I feel the slight unnatural puffiness there on that lovely Creamsicle lip, and I rush to banish that feeling. "This is not real."

She nods. A small pact is made.

"So, then," I say cheerily, "where would you like to have me, in the bed or the tub?"

If I'd figured to startle her, I had once again badly misfigured.

"Actually, the sink looks big enough," she chirps.

Life got so perfect so quickly. I love life for that.

In my pocket my phone buzzes me. Calls on my phone are so rare that I do reflexively pick up most of them right away.

"Jesus," I say, "my mother. I totally forgot. . . ."

I scurry into the other room, like one does to take a call privately. I come around the corner to find Junie sitting on the bed, giggling madly after having vaulted through the Japanese window.

"Jeez, Mom, I'm sorry," I say.

"That's it," Junie yells out. "We're moving here permanently."

I head back to the bathroom, and when I get there, Junie is standing on the bed, framed by the inter-room window, the big vista behind her providing the backdrop of purple sky and stars she should have with her always. She blesses me with a smile that makes me instantly feel like a far better guy than I will ever be able to be, and I feel an involuntary yip of love for her escape my lips.

"Okay, that was weird," Mom says as Junie slides the windows together to give us whatever privacy is possible. I hear the TV come on, which helps.

"So," I say, "how's it going?"

"You mean aside from getting my car stolen?"

"Come on, Mom. Of course you knew I didn't steal your car. But, yeah, I did kind of forget to bring it back."

"Or to call me."

"Sorry, sorry. I just got kind of preoccupied, when things got . . . hectic. Anyway, you knew I was over at Junie's"

I hear sounds in the background. Voices. Not my dad's. Female voices.

"Well, I *did* know that," she says.

"What's going on there?" I ask.

"Um, Son, do you really think this is a situation where you should be asking the questions?"

"Well, ah . . . Okay, good point."

"Oh, and what is this?" she says in that stage-whispery voice that signals to the person on the other end of the phone connection that she's not talking to them. "An appletini? Oh . . . Oh, oh my, that's luscious."

"Mom?" I say. "Right, I know I'm not supposed to be posing the questions, but what's going on there?"

"The girls are over," she says matter-of-factly.

"What girls?"

"The Blue girls. Leona and Maxine."

"You're kidding me?"

I hear her sipping. Slurping, actually.

"And you, young man, are at a *hotel*! With your princess bride." She goes into a small fit of giggles. "Whoops," she says.

"Whoops, what?"

"Maxine just spilled while topping up my 'tini."

"Tell Maxie to stop topping the 'tini," I demand. Demanding, I realize, is a trifle presumptuous.

"Oliver," Mom says in her very rare, very effective slap-the-young-man-down tone. She lets it hang for a moment while I achieve something resembling perspective.

"Okay, we're good," I say. "Nice party?"

"That would be far too strong a word, but under the circumstances, yes."

There is some instrumental jazz filling the air in the background as one of the ladies appears to have discovered the all-over-the-house audio system. Mom moves to another room, where the music still wafts but the guests do not.

"Leona wanted to come and thank me personally for her portrait," Mom says.

"Uh-huh. And Maxine had to accompany her."

"I think that was for the best."

"Leona drunk?"

"Not as drunk as I would be if I were her, but yes."

"Maxine chatty?"

"Oh, yes."

"That explains your hotel knowledge. What else do you know?"

"Nowhere near as much as I expect to know once I get back to the conversation. But that's another story. What more am I going to know once I finish with this conversation?"

"Um," I say tentatively, "not a whole lot?"

"Nnnn," she says. "I kind of figured as much. You realize, don't you, that I have every right to be furious and insulted and possibly panicked right now."

"Every right," I agree. "But don't panic."

She sighs. I hear distant voices seeking her out at my house.

"Will we pretend we have a normal relationship, and we just had a scalding argument, yelling and screaming about your thoughtlessness and selfishness and my controlling, misunderstanding, blah, blah, blah . . . without having to go through all that?"

"Perfect," I say. And she pretty much is.

"Whew, that was rough," she goofs. "I'm exhausted."

"Me too," I say. "You should probably get back to your party anyway, before Dad charms everybody right off their feet."

"Oh, he's not here. He's got one of those *things* tonight where he's boozing and charming people right off their wallets."

"He's a force," I say, suddenly worried that he might be doing all that right in this very building.

"Okay, but yes, I probably should get back to them," she says. Pause. Followed by pause. "Should I worry about you?"

"Under no circumstances."

"Okay. I will. For now, though, I will occupy myself with worrying about these two."

"They're good people, Mom."

"I know they are," she says.

"And so are you," I say.

"Well, duh," she says, laughs, and hangs up.

It is a source of great comfort that my mother says "duh" to me.

When I return to the bed, Junie is making that deep, full, pre-sleep breathing from somewhere deep within the fine sheets and comforter. The only part of her that is visible is her hand, which protrudes from the top, between the pillows. She has located the DO NOT DISTURB sign that you're supposed to hang on the doorknob, and she has secured it on the first two fingers of her hand. Clever girl.

I remove the sign, then notice on the reverse side a menu. *If you wish to preorder breakfast in your room, please fill out and hang on the outside of your door before three a.m.*

This sends me into something of a trance of preordered gluttony and thrill at the excitement of making this happen. By the time I hang the thing outside, it's as if somebody else has done it for me. I barely remember making the choices, and I don't recall what any of them are.

I just now realize how exhausted I am myself. I go around turning everything off, leave the curtains open to the stars and the waterfront, then crawl in under there with her. I am not bothered that I did not bring a toothbrush. Or anything else.

Who could be bothered by anything, here and now?

"You lied," she says, ever, ever so lightly, barely audibly.

I don't even want to know.

Eight

I awake to a dream.

That is, I believe I am awake, because I have never dreamed this well before, and even if it is a dream, then, well done, subconscious.

The sun is singing through the big window over the ocean, and Junie Blue is staring out at it, her back to me. I can smell the shower she has had, see her wet hair, see the white bathrobe she has on.

"Hey," I say.

She turns to face me. "Hey." She is smiling, shaking her head again.

"That's a nice robe," I say. It looks really thick and soft, like they took some extra duvet material and stuffed it inside a fluffy robe.

She walks to the side of the bed. "Feel it. This is the softest thing I have ever felt, including kittens."

I touch the sleeve of her garment, and it is indeed made of something like cloud.

"There's one for you, too, hanging on the back of the

bathroom door. They had notes attached, telling us to please enjoy them while we're here."

"Damn nice of them," I say.

"Damn nice. The shower is amazing."

"That, is good news," I say, hopping out of bed and trying to take advantage of momentum to kiss her. I don't get within five inches before she's onto me.

"You can use my toothbrush," she says from behind her hand. "It's in there."

I hop around to the shower and get right in. In the other room I hear the TV come on, and as I lather up with all the rich products on offer, things feel pretty serene. For a few minutes.

There is a knock on the door.

Junie freaks out entirely. She throws open the sliding windows again, and it feels like all the world, from Junie to the giant TV personalities sitting on the network couch, to everybody out there beyond our window, can see my nakedness.

"Somebody's at the door, the door," she shouts.

"So answer it."

"Yeah," she says, because June's antennae will always be more sharply tuned than mine, "what if it's my father? Or worse?"

That never even occurred to me, but at this point everything should occur to me.

"Who is it?" I shout.

"Room service," the man calls.

For a second it seems like she would have preferred her rampaging father.

"You ordered . . . what?"

I am feeling extremely naked right now, and not in the good way at all.

"Don't leave the man standing out there."

"Grrrr," she says at me, slams the sliders, and then goes to let him in.

I hear the rolling feast, the clattering of glasses and dishes, and try to remember the things I ordered. I hear brief polite discussion on both their parts, and eventually the gracious retreat of the room service gent.

The sliders fly open again.

"What is wrong with you?" she says.

I work feverishly to get all the lather off myself. "That's rhetorical, right?"

"Well, if you've got an actual answer, I will be fascinated to hear."

"Could you just . . . give me a minute here, Junie? I'll be right out."

"Fine," she says, slamming the sliders again.

Time passes, but not much of it. The amount of time it would take a person to, say, walk over and examine the contents of a room service breakfast for two, is what passes. Then the sliders whip open again.

"And for your next trick, apparently you plan to make me obese. What is *wrong* with you?"

"Rhetorical?"

"No. Have an answer for me when you come out."

She slams the windows again and, whether I should be or not, I am laughing to myself.

I walk cautiously out of the gilded bathroom of Caesar, into the carpeted, sunny main room, to find Junie sitting on the edge of the bed eating out of a basket of huge bursting red strawberries.

"*These* are okay," she says, sounding like she is needing to put effort into sounding peeved now.

I look over the delivery cart, which itself looks like one of the nicest restaurant tables I have seen, only on wheels.

"Wow," I say.

"'Wow,' is right," she says. "Madness."

"I'm kind of surprised myself, here in the bright light of day."

I scoop up a deep bowl containing three different kinds of fat grapes.

"What were you doing?" she says more calmly.

I pop a black seedless, and shrug. "Impress you?" I offer the bowl, and she peels off a bunch of the reds.

She sighs, but one of those big showy sighs where you make your lips push out and flap like a horse. Then she takes a strawberry and offers it right to my mouth.

If it were a strawberry, gooseberry, a shitberry, or a severed toe, I would still have taken it as she offered it. As it happens, it is the ripest, burstingest, most aromatic strawberry I have ever encountered. I make a groan of approval.

"I know," she says, on her third or fourth or whatever number it has taken to give her the world's reddest lips.

Partly due to my cajoling, partly due to profound hunger, and partly out of a horror of seeing things wasted, Junie eventually shares the bounty of this breakfast with me. There is far too much food, far too rich food, meats and pastries, eggs benedict with smoked salmon, coffee and Earl Grey tea, and the place smells better than any other place has ever smelled, and we do a heroic job of wasting as little as possible, but we finally surrender.

I wheel the corpse of breakfast out to the corridor, where the medics can collect it. Then I put the DO NOT DISTURB sign on the door properly, come back, and fall onto the bed, next to the girl, in front of the TV, immobilized with the effort of digestion. Bliss.

"So," she says, "how much did *that* cost?"

"Juuuune," I say sternly. "Remember. This is not real."

"It sure as hell isn't," she says.

"And nothing costs anything in this place that is unreal."
My torso is immobilized, but I gesture wildly in all directions
with my arms. "Money does not exist here on our planet. It
is a planet powered by thought. We think it, it happens. We
wish it, it materializes."

"Yeah? This's quite a planet we have."

"Yes indeed," I say leaning closer into her, even though
I was already leaning right up against her. "Guess what I am
wishing now?"

"Oh. Jeez, well, so much for the planet, huh, because that
won't be materializing."

Wow. That was thorough.

"Are you trying to tell me I just destroyed an entire planet
with my . . . quest?"

"Sure, but don't sweat it. Why should you be the one to
break the unbroken chain of men throughout human history?"

We both lie there in silence, the TV nattering away while
we give that statement the fear and respect it deserves.

"That was pretty scathing," I venture.

"Good, you got it, then. I was afraid, being a guy and all . . ."

"Wait," I say brightly. "Silver lining. Glass half-full. What
I get from that is, if somehow I *am* the man to break that
chain, then I'm sure to get some."

"Yes," she says, matching my brightness, "but then you'll

be thinking that way, you will reveal yourself as such, and it's *back* on the chain gang for you, mister."

"Argghh," is my final word on the subject.

She laughs full-throatedly at me.

In frustration and fun I fling myself sideways off the bed and bounce up again in what is becoming my default position, pleading—okay, begging—praying, folded hands and everything.

"Not sure I'm liking this new move of yours as much as maybe I should. Did you retreat to your old altar boy gig when I dumped you or something? Because I don't think I could live with that."

"I miss this *so much*, Junie. I miss it *so much*."

"So do I, O."

"Then let's just stop missing it. Look." I grab the lapels of my bathrobe, and it's like grabbing a whipped cream jacket. "Look, look at our robes. Look at our big window. Look!"

"What? I mean, what?"

"I don't know. I have no idea what I mean by that, but I'm just spotting the nicest things in the room and roping them in to help me."

I am making her laugh, which has to be a good thing, always was a good thing when there were good things. She leans over and takes my altar boy hands, and pulls me up onto the bed like she has landed a big tuna and is hauling it into her boat.

"You, are the nicest thing in the room, Oliver," she says, and pulls me into her bed.

When we wake up—well, when Junie wakes up, since I never fully fell back to sleep but lay there smelling her hair—she speaks first.

"I'll getcha back," she says quietly.

When I remain speechless, she rolls over to regard me up close. If my face is not lying, it speaks of puzzlement.

"Okay," I say. "It seems to me there are a number of ways to take that statement. Could be 'I'll get you back,' like when one person pays for lunch or something and the other one pledges to return the favor. Or there's the more intense 'I'll get you back,' like when one person does something foul and reprehensible to another and then there is the possibility that it's more along the lines of, 'I'll get your back,' like, 'If you're ever in need, I'll be there.'

"Anyhow you look at it, that's a hell of a thing to wake up to, Ms. Blue."

She slap-claps a hand over my mouth, kisses my nose, and says, "It was absolutely not the second one." Then she climbs over me on her way to the bathroom. I hear the magnificent shower get its third outing of the day.

My phone rings, and I cross the room all spritely to answer it. I answer with a very silly, "Yell-o."

"Well, that's my *first* question answered. Congratulations, boy."

"Maxine, what are you doing on my mother's phone?"

"It was the first one I saw when I woke up."

"And where did you wake up?"

"Your living room."

"You guys slept over at my house?"

"I did. I don't know if the other two have gone down at all yet. Lots of art going on in this house, and lots of chatter. Ronny even made a raucous appearance on your front lawn, until your father made a phone call that made Ronny disappear. That was cool. Wish I had that number."

"My dad called the police?"

"Didn't look like police to me."

"Is my dad there now?"

"Come and gone again. Awfully businesslike, that man."

"That would be him, yes. Are you calling me for any special reason?"

There is an uncharacteristic Maxie silence on the line.

"Max?"

"I believe her, O. In fact, everybody in this house right now believes her. But nobody gives a shit what we believe. And perceptions, some places more than others—perceptions matter. People think she's hiding something, and with certain people there is nothing, like nothing, that sets them off more than that feeling. And she's too tough for her own good, uncompromising, pig— Well, you know."

"Oh, do I know."

"Right. So . . . best keep her away just yet. Keep her away. At least another day."

"Done." I say, bravely accepting the happiest assignment of my life. "What then, though?"

"I don't know," she says. "Another day? Then another day after that? I don't know. All I know is today. All I know is I love the crazy little freakin' bat, and you need to keep her today. You can do that."

"I can."

"All right. I'm gonna go check on the other bats and see what's goin' on here. Don't be surprised at all the batshit you find when you come home."

"Charming," I say, and she hangs up on a laugh.

"Who you braggin' to?" Junie says as she comes out of the bathroom. "Guys. Don't even wait for the testicles to cool down before they're waving them around town for all the other rutting pigs to see."

I know how she can be, but still.

"That was appalling," I say.

"You're damn cute when you're appalled," she says, "but I have to go."

"What?" I jump up when she drops her bathrobe, revealing herself fully clothed in shorts and a button-down short-sleeved shirt. "We're just getting started."

"I have things to do, O. I have to work. Real world returns, guy."

"Well, just make it go away."

"Careful," she says in a voice and with a pointedly pointed finger that suggests I'd really better be. "You're highlighting our, ahem, *situational* differences again. I gotta *work*, I told you. I can't just *make it go away*. And you know what else? I *want* to work."

"The shop? Christ, you can't go into the shop, not today."

"I got no idea what you have against the shop all of a sudden, but it ain't the shop today. It's the dogs. I got four different houses that are going to be craptastic by the time their owners get home if I do not fulfill my obligations. And I, junior, am a woman who takes her obligations seriously."

I had not planned for this. I had not, actually, planned for any bumps in my glowing yellow-brick road.

"But we're booked for two nights," I say.

"So, unbook one."

Rats.

"Ah, we'll lose that second night's money."

She sly-smiles me. "I thought money didn't exist here, in our world, on our planet?"

Mopping the floor with me, she is.

I walk to the big window and watch the boats in the harbor. I do not doubt for a second that, like the fancy boats under the stars last night, the dashing vessels under the glorious sunshine today are all just part of what a place like this can arrange for aesthetic purposes. It's *all* about money. Of course it is. Everything is.

Suddenly her arms are around my waist, and she's looking at the same all-that-glitters as I am.

"I can't let you lose what you paid," she says. "I just can't do that. One more night."

O-kay. Lyin' O'Brien pulls it off. Just.

I turn around and hug her.

"Can I say something?" I ask.

"Oh, God," she says, and squinches her eyes tight shut.

"I'll drive you," I say.

After a brief hesitation she opens her eyes and lets out an awkward laugh of relief.

"What?" I say. "What? What were you afraid I was going to say?"

"Huh? What? I don't know. Nothing. I don't even remember. Let's just get going."

"Right," I say, heading to the bathroom with my clothes to pull myself together. "I'll drop you out there and then pick you up again later."

"Great," she says as I close the bathroom door.

I burst like Bugs Bunny through the sliders. "I do love you, though," I say, and then slam them again quickly and cowardly.

"Dammit, dammit," I hear her say, and for whatever reason this gives me wonderful satisfaction.

When I drop her off at her first assignment, she hands me a folded sheet of eight-by-ten paper, on which she has drawn a fairly convincing map of the neighborhood. On it she has highlighted all the addresses where she has dog contracts, and circled the one where she will be finishing the day.

"I basically have to do two loops. Each stop, I check on 'em, make sure they are fed and watered, walk them, then move on to the next place. Then I do it the same for all the others, double back around, and walk them all once more. It's more than it sounds, actually. Takes a few hours."

"Great. I will meet you there, at four. I'll pick you up and take you home with me."

My delight at saying this is too obvious for my own good.

"Maybe we should think about getting a dog of our own," I add.

She closes the passenger side door and leans back in on the window.

"You know we're just playing house, O."

"But what a house, huh?" I say, pointing at her.

"And what play, huh?" she says, pointing back. She's probably just being kind. I probably don't care.

I drive away, bobbing my head along with a jazz radio station my mother apparently likes, my smile and my agenda firmly in place.

I knock on the door.

"Malcolm, what the hell are you doing here?" I say.

He stares at me.

"You look like a fool, boy," I tell him.

He stares at me.

"In training for that gig you've always dreamed about— tennis star in the daytime and gangster doorman at night?"

In a snap Malcolm disappears from my sight, yanked out of the way as Ronny appears.

"And you want . . . what?" he says.

"What were you doing at my house last night?"

"What were my women doing at your house last night? And today?"

"Is something atrocious going to happen to me if my answer is 'Demonstrating good taste'?"

He smiles. The smile of a man who does not wish one good tidings.

"You got friends, little man. That's nice."

"You'll find that most good people have friends."

"And you will find that no matter how many friends you have, if you make *one more* wiseass remark to my face, on my doorstep, I don't care what happens, you're gonna wind up with your nuts in your mouth."

I thought I had something going there. I actually felt ascendant.

He leans my way, stares bug-eyed. "Response?"

I take a deep breath. Fortunately, my wiseass just broke.

"Leave Junie alone."

Even the air has come to a standstill here.

"Rules must be followed. Respect must be paid. If your little girlfriend is too ignorant to work that out, then she'll pay some other way. She'll get no grief from me. But she'll get no help from me neither."

He makes a washing-hands gesture, then spits, on his own step, between my feet, before slamming the door in my face.

I smell incense mixing with the usual flowers as I walk up the path to my house. That same jazz station is filling the air inside.

I walk around inside quietly, just to see what I can see without being seen.

I see Maxine asleep on the couch, so I don't bother her. I go from living room to kitchen to dining room, where I find an absolute riot of artwork. Sketches, pastels, watercolors, some tacked up on the walls, several canvases propped on easels, some charcoal drawings laid out, on different sheets, lined up like moveable puzzle pieces on the dining room table. Much of this work is recognizably Mom's, but much of it is way, way outside the regular track. It's figurative, and not, and it reminds me of the Leonardo Da Vinci Grotesques exhibit Mom saw a couple years ago and raved about for . . . a couple of years. She spoke about it with admiration and awe and excitement and abject fear. Never, to my knowledge, attempted to go there with her own art before. I get a full-body chill and have to leave the room.

I look out the kitchen window, and there, side by side in the dirt, are Mom and Leona, gardening.

"I'm never leaving here," Max says, making me nearly leap through the window with shock.

"Jesus, Maxine."

"I love this place. Love, love, love your mom."

"You know you have part of a tuna sandwich stuck to the underside of your arm?" I say.

She doesn't even move it. "I love tuna," she says.

"Are you stoned?" I ask, laughing.

"No," she says firmly, smiling. "I'm blissed. And blessed. This place is blessed."

I walk past her, heading up to my room to get a few things. She follows behind.

"It does have a certain vibe, I guess," I say, "though I'm not sure it was exactly here before you guys showed up."

"Good. How's June?"

"June is aces. She is just working for a few hours, and then I'll be picking her up again."

"Working? Aw, Christ, not the dog thing. I'll tell you what, if it turned out she did win the lottery and was still picking up animal shit with her hands, I would personally beat her to death with a rawhide bone."

I pause from stuffing clothes and toiletries into an overnight bag. "There's that vibe again, huh?"

"Seriously, though. The vibe exists. Maybe when things cool down, bring June back here. We'll all live here—you, me, your mom, my mom, Junie. It'll be like a commune. Like a true feminist paradise, and the men can just all go to hell."

I zip my bag closed with all the manly gusto I can manage.

"I'm going to go now," I say.

I drive back downtown, back to the hotel. As I pull up and the doorman rushes right over, greets me like an old pal, yet a superior one, takes my money and my keys, I have to confess I am feeling this.

Without that thing that June Blue brings to this situation, a thing I suppose some might call perspective, others might call shame, I start to enjoy this position I'm in.

I take my modest little bag toward the elevator, then have a brilliant thought. I go to the desk for a very crisp and lean conversation, like I was born doing this kind of thing.

"Flowers?" I say to the man.

"Excellent," he says and smiles. "Roses?"

"Sounds about right."

"Color?"

"What are the choices?"

"More than you might think."

I shrug. "A variety?"

"Yes, sir. Would you like a dinner reservation?"

"Uh . . . don't think so. Don't want to push it. We'll find something."

"Subtlety is a gift, sir. Beautiful summer day, though, is it not?"

"It is."

"Have we considered a harbor cruise?"

"We have not, but we are now."

"Time?"

"Um, what time is sunset?"

"I will check, and I will book, and I will have the confirmation sent to your room."

I am excited enough to really give myself away here. I must calm down.

"Where have you been all my life?" I say to the man.

"Right here behind this desk the whole time, Mr. O'Brien."

"Ha." I shake his hand and sashay on up to my room.

I am standing at my big window, staring out over the breath-taking bay, looking at all the fine watercraft coming and going, one of them coming for us. This is *it*, isn't it?

"Are you *nuts?*"

I am thinking it, and saying it out loud, as if to prove the nutsness, as if it needs more proving.

Pointless ostentation, yup, that is the surest way to the heart of this woman. Show her the shallowness she has always expected like a trapdoor waiting to open onto the bottomless world of greed and awfulness.

But it's a *boat*.

And flowers. Don't forget flowers.

Okay. I do not know what I am doing. I am flailing, is what I am doing. I am so desperate to have Junie—the live and unharmed and *here* version of her—in my life, and all the way in, that there isn't a notion so crazy that it doesn't at least get to the interview stage.

But even if I interview them all, tomorrow is still coming. And when it does, what is all your money going to—

Jeeee-zuz.

What a moron. What a solid-gold, triple-A-rated fool have I been to not figure out the straightest, simplest solution to the source of everyone's happiness, when it has been waving its aromatic tail feathers under my nose all the time?

That is a rhetorical question.

Some ideas are just too right, too perfect, to stop and think about them.

I hit the marble floor running, skittering across the lobby, out the front doors, left, and left again toward the financial district, through throngs of power-suited dopes and dopettes. I am sweating like a plow beast when I reach the front doors of my dad's office building.

I take the elevator up to Dad's floor, step off, and grin like a maniac at his receptionist, who tells me he is on a conference call, if I want to take a seat. I do not want at all to take a seat, because I am too anxious, so I go straight into nutty pacing mode, which is not nutty at all for me when I am feeling this way in my own house, but here and now, with me dripping sweat all over the nice burgundy carpets and practicing what I want to say to my father, surely has this poor woman on the verge of triggering whatever security gizmo she has back there, when my father comes out probably just in time.

"Oliver!" Dad says, genuinely surprised and thrilled to see me. We hug, and he hauls me down the hall to his office.

I should be able to do small talk here, or large talk, or at least humanity-based father-son talk, but I am a maniac on a mission.

"I have to ask a favor, Dad."

"Oooo," he says, leaning back in his chair, not serious, exactly, but definitely attentive. "You don't often—"

"Ever," I point out quickly, figuring this point may become rather vital.

"Pretty much never," he says. "So, you've got my attention, Son."

"Money," I say.

"Money," he says.

I nod. Nod, nod, nod, nod.

"All right," he says, laughing. "Money. So . . ."

"Could you, if I needed you to, transfer some money into my account, like instantly, so I could write a check on it?"

I have no idea what is in this account, because I have never needed to know. Never wanted to either. I have one account that I can get cash out of with my bank card, that I consider *my* account. And then there's the other account that he manages for me that is some kind of convoluted checking-savings-investment-interest-bearing spaceship of a thing that orders Chinese food for itself and keeps my room clean. I carry two of those checks folded up in my wallet for absolute-absolute emergencies, and otherwise we have nothing to do with each other.

"Well, not instantly exactly, but fairly quickly. Are you going to tell me what for?"

I smile and blink at him all coy and realize how lucky I
am to be an only child so that this kind of thing might still
work on him. Sisters would surely have killed this for the
likes of me by this point in my life.

"Not if you don't force me to."

It's not the coy. It's because he loves me.

"No, I won't be forcing you to. Are you going to—God
help us—give me the figure? Agreeable as I would like to be,
it would be hard to do this without that."

I swallow hard, hear myself gulp, which makes Dad laugh
sympathetically.

"Can I have that?" I say, pointing to his cube of notepaper
with its own pen holder.

"That bad, huh?" he says, pushing it across the desk.

I take the pad, and I write down the figure I'm thinking
of. As I push the pad back across the desk, I say, "But before
you look, I want you to know the bright side. This is just a
loan. You can take it back gradually. Out of my paycheck."

He has the pad right under his nose now, but doesn't
look. He looks across at me and goes all wide-eyed silly, like
an older version of my dizziest self.

"Really?" he says.

I nod.

"Son." He gasps a tiny bit. "Son, I am so happy. I will
teach you everything, and I mean everything."

"I am crap with numbers, Dad."

"Pfft," he says. "I can't even count. We pay people for that. I can't ever pay somebody for the trust, the trust I will have in you. I will show you. You will shadow me. You will be my shadow, and this will begin the greatest . . ."

He looks at the figure.

"You'll pay me back out of your pay."

"Uh-huh."

"Uh-huh. For the next twenty-five years?"

My heart sinks. I feel sick, I feel humiliated.

He looks up at me, grinning. "Jeepers, O, you're not going to cry, are you? Don't spoil everything now. I am thrilled that we're going to be working together. You and me. Forever. Take that look off your face. For the love of God, you're going to make *me* start bawling."

He crumples up the paper and throws it into the wastebasket.

"You're not going to make the transfer?" I say.

"No," he says.

I nod. I stand up and offer to shake his hand. He refuses to take it, because he is not finished turning me inside out.

"There's no need, because the money's already in there."

I *fall* back into my chair.

"The money is *what*?"

"In there."

"Are you *kidding* me?"

"No."

He gets calmer the more wigged-out I get.

"That much money? Is, and was, in my account."

"Sure," he says. "Hey, just because you don't want to be taken care of doesn't mean I can't take care of you if I damn well please."

We are in one of those rare cosmic moments when two people with wildly different outlooks are converging on something and making each other very, very happy over some uncommon ground.

"You are really enjoying this, aren't you?" I say.

"Uh-huh," he says. "And admit it, so are you."

I want to defend myself and tell him, *Well, I am enjoying something unseemly but for a very good reason*, but that would require a discussion of the reason, which would not be good, and the fact is, the basic truth of his statement is beyond dispute.

"For this moment," I say, standing up and shaking his hand, "I am enjoying your money."

"Hah," he says. "But it's *our* money. Not bad for the root of all evil, huh?"

He comes around the desk, walks me down the hall with his arm over my shoulders, and waits for the elevator with me.

"Sally," he crows to the receptionist, "this is my shadow. He will be shadowing me in the future, and someday this will all be his."

Dear God, where am I? Dear God, where is the elevator?

"Looking forward to working with you, Mr. Shadow," Sally says as my dad playfully shoves me into the gaping elevator.

Mr. Shadow. My father casts a shadow, and it is me.

What have I done?

Well, nothing, yet.

I run again, from Dad's financial district office building to my hotel at the seaport, sprouting a whole new sheen of sweat before I jump back into the car. I tear off for my town again as I flip through the radio presets.

One thing I have discovered, living so much in my mother's car, is that her jazz station calms me some. It will never be my station of full-time, full-on engagement, but right now it is just the right accompaniment as I head back up the parkway, watching the road and reading Junie's little street map at the same time.

It's twenty past three, well ahead of schedule for picking her up from her last assignment. If I time it right, maybe I can make that final walk around the blocks with her. I like that. I like this.

I quick-scan the map in between glances at the road. Don't see any problems. I know where it is. I start looking at the other houses on the map—that's the one with the boxers, then Archie the antisocial Airedale, and then there's—

A bellowing truck horn pulls my attention to the road, and I pull my vehicle back to my side of it. It is a notorious stretch, this, beautiful with the pond on the right and the stately houses on the left, but it is crazy winding, was made for much more civilized traffic and should be three times as wide as it is now. Respect and attention must be paid here.

But the map. I have figured all the clients out but one. And I consider the neighborhood where it's located.

I drop the map onto the seat, and I barrel toward the home of Bam, the Boston baboon-ass terrier.

Nine

I stand on the porch of the plain, postwar box of a house. Faded yellow vinyl siding and everything. I am shaking, which is fine except if it shows, so I fight it. I ring the doorbell, and the dog tries to bark, but he even *oooks* like a tiny ape.

"You gotta be kidding me," is the proprietor's greeting. "What are you doing here?"

"I'm here to walk the dog," I say.

He pushes open the screen door and ushers me past as he holds it for me. "My dog walker is a lot prettier than you, I can tell you that."

"Okay, I lied," I say, once I'm in.

"You shouldn't lie. A good kid like you especially, you shouldn't lie."

Five seconds in and I already feel played.

I need to get in and get out, minimize the damage.

Five minutes later we are seated at his old Formica kitchen table. There is strong coffee in small cups in front of us, and a plate of biscotti. Biscotti are awful unless you have good coffee, in which case they are magic.

The dog is at my feet staring up at me. His face looks like a mangled shoe that he himself might have chewed beyond recognition.

The house is extremely comfortable: simple, homey, from what I can see. Artwork on the walls and shelves fall into three categories—family photos, Eastern Orthodox iconography painted onto wood, and one framed picture of Vladimir Putin sitting shirtless on a horse. I am aware I have been staring.

He's looking right at me, sipping his coffee behind grinning, knowing eyes. He's been allowing me to take in the scene, encouraging it, in fact.

"You like my house?"

"Ah, I do. Yes, very much."

"You were expecting more, though. Opulence or something."

"Um, no, sir. No expectations of any kind."

"You'd be the first, then. Truth is, I raised three kids and two wives under this roof, fixed them up nice and set them all free. Couldn't imagine living anywhere else."

"It's a fine house."

"Not as nice as your house, though. But very few are."

Get in, get out. Don't play. Jesus, he's scary.

Except, of course, he's not. He's not anything. He's not big, but not small, either. I thought he'd be older. He's none of those things you expect to find with these guys—

you know, either brutal and menacing or very grandfatherly and faux sweet. I have seen him a few times, from a bit of a distance and in photographs. But I barely recognize this guy from those. His features are what you would call pleasant, as is his voice, as are his gestures.

Maybe I have seen him more than a few times. Maybe thousands.

And I can almost bet that if I saw him tomorrow, I might walk right past him again without noticing.

I drink my coffee and eat two biscotti. He pours me a second cup without my asking.

"It's not too strong, is it? Sometimes I forget, and when I stand up, I'm bouncing off the walls."

"No, sir, some of the best coffee I've ever had."

"Ah, flattery," he says, waving me off.

We sit, stare, and sip, until it can't really go on anymore.

"So, I have to be rude and ask, to what do I owe the pleasure of your company this lovely summer's day? If I were your age—if I were *you*, especially—the last place I would be spending my time would be in a dark house with a dull old man."

I place my coffee cup down in its saucer. It makes the telltale clinking sound of the hand of the nervous young man. Also, the coffee was pretty damn strong.

"I won the lottery," I say. I intended to be ultra-cool with the delivery, but it still came out like one slurred word. *Iwonulodery.*

Not that I am any kind of expert on such things, but I would imagine this is a very difficult man to startle. And, not that I would have anything to measure him by, I am guessing that the wide-eyed, two-hands-up-like-surrender pose I am seeing represents startle in this house.

"You?" he says evenly, coming rapidly back to composure.

"Me."

"You? Not anybody else? That is quite a thing, what with the winning ticket having been sold out of the very shop your lovely lady works at."

"I know. What are the odds, right? But that's lottery stuff for ya, long odds and all. So, yeah, me. Nobody else. Oh. Except, obviously, you."

He lets out a little laugh, reaches across and pats one of my hands in, yes, a grandfatherly way.

"I have to say, I don't know what to make of you at all, mister," he says.

"I hope I'm not out of line in saying pretty much the same thing about you."

"Not at all, not at all. That's a good thing, is it not? The problem is with perceptions. You know, in any town, whispers start. Whispers become perceptions, become rumors, become accepted fact and legend, when in reality hardly five percent of that kind of thing is ever true. A guy, a local guy who's a successful businessman, because he's maybe a tough competitor, and because most small-timers can't figure out what makes him consistently good at what he does, they make up these boogey man stories that become the official record in people's minds."

I am listening. But I am not nodding or grunting or doing anything committal, because I frankly have no idea what to commit to. This, I think, shows.

"What?" he says.

Can't take anything for granted here. I consider what kind of offer "What?" might be.

"Cards on the table?" I say.

"Face up."

"The official record is that you are ruthless, maybe to the point of brutality. It says you do not care what it takes, you are going to have your success, your way, and you do not care what happens to rivals, nor what anybody thinks."

He folds his hands in front of his mouth, and looks to be descending into some deeper thought place. "That I find offensive. I have to say, I don't blame you for starting that kind of talk, because I know you are just the messenger, and I appreciate your directness. But I care very, very much what people think. What *good* people think of me, people like you, and your good lady—that matters to me as much as anything. I have worked as hard as any man ever has, to take care of his family, and I have done a very good job of that, if you'll indulge my boasting a little there. I am no saint, true enough, but my money, I assure you, is *clean*. Like any real man, I do what needs to be done. That's all. I submit that I have done a lot more good for this community than bad."

"Okay," I say. "But how does somebody measure a thing like that? What's the gauge?"

"Easy. The people. The people are always the gauge. Ask them."

"Who? Which people do you ask?"

He smiles a checkmate smile.

"The good ones, of course."

"Oh, right," I say. "Like good Ronny Blue."

And here, up from the depths without any warning, is the ruthless, chilling creature of legend.

"*That* dog," he says, leaning hard across the table and showing me every one of his sixty pointed teeth. "A dog like that, I feed occasionally, scraps from my fine table, to get him to bite somebody who needs biting. So he's a well-fed dog, but a dog nonetheless. He sniffs around; makes noise, does stupid, ignorant stunts that are supposed to impress me, when he is the exact opposite of what I am all about. I tell you this, kid, you ever hear that sonofabitch even mention my name, you are authorized to call me personally and then stand by to watch me choke the stinking bastard to death with his own thong."

I almost choke on that last part right now.

"So," I say when his breathing slows some, "you don't like him."

He smiles, but it is a bit of an effort. Something transformative has happened, sort of a genie partway out of a bottle and stuck there for the time being.

"You need to get to your point now, Oliver," he says, somewhat chillingly.

I pull out my wallet, pull out the check.

"The thing is, sir, while I won the lottery, I lost the ticket."

He says nothing. Stares at me, into me, beyond me by several generations.

"But that's not your problem. That's for me to deal with. Rules must be followed, respect paid." I write the check with a shaky hand as I talk. My phone starts ringing. Excellent timing, phone. It rings on. I realize that while I am aware of multiple names for the man, I have no idea what the real one is. "Who should I make this out to?"

"Harry," he says.

I write "Harry," then look up to him. There will be nothing else forthcoming.

"Harry, it is," I say. I hand over the check, and while he's looking at it, I say, "Obviously that's just the first installment. There will be plenty more until we're all right."

He says nothing. Phone rings again. I stand, he stands,

the dog stands. We all walk to the front door, and when I am outside, I realize the last word I heard him say was "Harry."

I should not be driving.

My heart is bu-booming so hard, it is surely going to trigger the air bag, which will break every bone in my head and make me crash and die.

The conversation, the caffeine—I feel drugged, but that is probably just another nuts reaction to where I've been—the fear, and as it all sets in, the reality of the magnitude of what I have just accomplished makes me dangerously supercharged behind the wheel.

I screech to a stop at the house where June Blue sits scowling on the front steps.

"How can you be so late, driving so fast?" she asks as we zoom away from the curb.

"Really, really sorry. I'll make it up to you, though."

"Make it up to me by slowing down, right now," she says, her hands braced up against the glove compartment.

"Sorry. How was your day, then? Good? Looking forward to getting home? Hey, this is like we're married, huh, chatting about the day, you criticizing my driving . . ."

"Seriously, O, calm it down or let me off. I mean it. What have you been taking, anyway?"

"Nothing, I swear. Just really great coffee and a general lust for life, is all."

I can feel her staring at me, suspicious. I still can't help smiling.

It feels like I have done something heroic. And we are going to celebrate.

We can smell them in the hallway before we even open the door to the room.

"Wow," Junie says, her nose in the air like a retriever. "Heavenly. You smell that?"

"I do indeed," I say, and throw open the door for her.

They are at the far end of the room, on the desk right by the window.

"Oh, my," she says, and walks straight for the roses.

As fine as my mother's garden is, I have never seen anything like this. They are like a floral fireworks explosion. There are deep velvety red roses, pink ones, yellow, white, fuchsia, and some that are swirly combinations of two or three colors in the same bloom. There must be two dozen.

She buries her face in them, even though you could probably pick up the scent down in the underground parking garage.

"What are these doing here?"

"I guess they like having you around."

"*They* do, do they?" she says. She is trying to get tough with me, and largely succeeding, but the flowers are intoxicating, even for me. Go, flowers.

She plucks a yellow rose out of the bunch, pulls out the desk chair, and turns it around to face me as she sits.

"Truly, O," she says, breathing the scent deeply, "this is stunning, gorgeous, sweet, and unnecessary. It's not going to change one single thing. You know that. The fantasy—as mind-blowing a fantasy as it's been—will close tomorrow morning. It will slam shut tomorrow morning."

"I know that," I say casually, walking past her and scooping an envelope off the desk, which I open at the window with my back to her.

"You know it, but I'm not certain you *know* it, know it."

It is our reservation on the evening cruise.

"I know it, know it, know it," I say to her with enough enthusiasm to make her more suspicious, not less.

She sighs dramatically. "Lucky for you I'm a sad, pathetic sucker for flowers, which you well know."

"Which I well do."

"Or I'd make you send them back," she says, pulling a pink and white bloom out to admire with the yellow one.

"I know. So, are you hungry?"

She stands up, walks right over to me, and starts bouncing the flowers off my face like they're some sort of judge's gavel. "You are relentless. You don't need to do anything else. I will be perfectly satisfied and entertained just by spending another night in this carnival of decadence right here."

"Uh-huh," I say. "But you have to eat. Everybody has to eat."

"Y'know, not necessarily. After this morning's breakfast I don't think I need to eat for another three or four days."

"Oh, come on n—"

She waits for just the right moment, and jams a rose right into my gaping mouth.

"There," she says, satisfaction smiling. "Now you've eaten. I," she adds with a flourish, "would not be able to forgive myself if I left here without sampling that glorious bath. Which I am going to do right now."

I give her back her rose. "That, is a capital idea."

"Yes," she says on the way to get it started. "But if you get any capital ideas, say, involving that window between the bathroom and bedroom, you will have far worse rose-orifice troubles to come. Thorns and all. And your mouth will be the least of your worries."

I am going to have to do a cost-benefit analysis of taking that risk.

Cripes, I'm thinking like my father's shadow already.

One point of the multiple taps must be to jet the massive tub full of water with fire-hose efficiency, because well before I expected, I hear the taps off and Junie splashing around in there. Then I hear a major, theatrical "Ahhhhh."

"Everything it's cracked up to be?" I ask, sitting on the

bed with my back up against the headboard. Basically sharing a communal wall with her as she bathes, while I stare out across at the sky through the window wall.

"Everything," she says.

"I'm glad."

"Listen, you can open the window."

"Really?" I say excitedly.

"For communicating, O, not for ogling. If you peek, we're back to the old arrangement with you pulling rose stems out of your ass."

"Junie Blue," I say, aghast.

"Yeah, yeah," she says, giggling.

I turn around, reach up, and move the sliders apart. My head remains safely below the parapet, while my hands rejoice, like a puppet show. "Hi," I say, waving at her with both of them.

"Hi," she says.

I sit back down with my back to her and my eyes focused out over the harbor.

"I'm not sure if it's coming across very well, but I truly appreciate all this. I mean, really, really," she says.

"It's coming across just fine. Anyway, you're well aware I'm happy to do it. It's kind of selfish on my part, if you really want to examine it closely, which I'm hoping you don't."

A spritz stream of water arcs over the dividing wall and lands in my lap.

"No, it's not," she says. "You care about me."

"How did you do that? Did you bring a water pistol to a fancy hotel, and into the fancy bath? Because if you did that, then I have a whole new level of respect and devotion to you that I'm afraid you are going to find very hard to cope with."

She laughs, and another spritz lands exactly on top of the first. I look very much like a guy who has just had an accident, making for great cover, since something like that is entirely possible right now.

"It's that clam thing, where you cup your hands together and squirt the water out from between the heels of your thumbs."

"I could never do that. How 'bout you show me?"

"You're cute," she says.

"I'm trying very hard not to be."

We are both laughing now, the kind of easy bippity-boppity-boo we used to do all the time.

I am aching for her right now. Not just aching for the physical her—though, that is well represented too—but for *her*. For us, for this.

With almost no physical distance between us, I have never been so lonely.

"Is this what one might call an ominous silence?" she says.

It's almost like a wheezing sensation, a constriction holding me from midchest to middiaphragm, making me a little nervous to talk because I fear it has a sound as well.

"Ominous sounds too big," I say. To me it sounds like a wheeze. "How 'bout 'awkward.'"

"Too late. The silence is already gone, so it's neither."

The mist from the bath is wafting out of there and into here. It settles over me like a fog, and I breathe it in. It's the smell of steam, which I love anyway, mixed with the roses and the fancy bath elements the hotel provided and June applied. I close my eyes and have it, and commit to keep it, this olfactory memory, this essence of Junie.

"Why are we not together?" I blurt.

And I wait.

"Will we call this one ominous?" she says.

"I suppose," I say.

"I'm leaving, sweetheart," she says, using a term she has used three times ever on me, and brought me to my knees three times. "I have to go away."

"No, you don't."

The water spritzes. She's really expert at this.

"I do."

"Is my crotch going to get even wetter if I ask why?"

"I guess that's up to you, weirdo."

"I didn't mean . . . Right, why do you feel like you have to go?"

"Do you love me enough to listen to my clichés, then?"

"It is what it is."

"That's the spirit. Well, I have to leave, to find out who I want to be, what I want to be. All I know from being here is, I know what I don't want to be, or maybe what I can't be. I can't be one of your people. I can't. I'm sorry, O, but you folks are just like martians to me. And if I have to be one of my people, I'll kill myself. I love my mother, love my sister, but I want my life to be as different from theirs as leopards are from frogs. I don't even know what's possible. I need to see what's possible. It's not even something I've worked out in my head, exactly. It's just something I *know*. Like when you have to eat, you *know*, and that's how I know this."

Every manner of silence now floats like the Junie Blue mist in the room. I hear small swishes in the water.

"O? Oliver?"

"How come you never told me that before?"

"I don't know. I have no idea. I guess I was never in this bathtub before. And you were never right on the other side of that wall under the sliding communal bedroom-bathroom Japanese frosted glass window thingy before."

I decide to take the high road.

"Stupid room. I knew there was something I hated about this stupid room."

"Ah. I expected you to take it graciously, and you didn't let me down. And anyway, maybe I'll come back. Maybe I'll find out that every place and everybody is just as rotten as here, except worse because they don't have you. Then I'll come back for sure. But I can't come back if I don't leave first."

"The hunger thing."

"Yeah, that."

"So, are you ready to go out for food yet?"

"Ha. Would you like that?"

"Yes."

"Okay. Close them damn sliders and let a girl get ready already."

Once again I am pushing with all my might in a direction I know is not going to get us anywhere.

"The seafood place just a couple of wharves up from here is just incredible." I am being more provocative than serious. "The chowder is famous, but I tell you, the lobster roll—"

"Lobster?" She laughs right in my face.

"Yeah. And I'll get a whole lobster myself, so they'll make me wear one of those plastic bibs with a lobster picture on it, and you'll laugh at me the whole meal. It'll be fantastic."

She is shaking her head, shaking her head. We have just stepped out of the water-side entrance to our hotel. It is that time of day when the sun's just beginning to give up, the light angling lower and skipping gold across the top of the water. The same gold glints off every shiny bit of every shiny boat decorating the harbor just for us. I have our reservations in my back pocket.

"I have to tell ya, O, I am really exhausted. Not only would I never bite into a lobster even if it bit me first—"

"Mostly they pinch, more than bite. I don't think they even have teeth—"

"I don't want to go two wharves down. I don't want to go to that next wharf right there either if I can help it. What's wrong with here?"

The answer to that is, there is nothing in the world wrong with here. In front of us, like a glorious patio opening out from the hotel all the way down to the water's edge, is a fine-looking outdoor establishment that is actually just another outlet of the hotel's own endless provision of goods and services. Small circular white tables are dotted all around, waitstaff gliding back and forth between the inside kitchen and the island bar set right in the middle of it all. Parasols protect each intimate little group from the elements, which right now amount to a sea breeze you would pay a thousand dollars for if they would bottle it, and the first bits of red hinting at the coming sunset.

"Classic, isn't it?" I say as the waitress leads us down to a nice spot not twenty feet from the water. "We're always look-ing for paradise two wharves away when we have our own lovely pier right under our nose."

We sit across from each other with the hotel to one side of us and the ocean to the other.

"Wharf wisdom?" she says to me.

"I'm thinking of writing a book."

"Good. That'll keep you busy."

The waitress is back with us, bearing glasses of ice water.

"Any chance of a beer?" I ask with a smile.

"Any chance of an ID?" she responds with a better smile.

"Ha," Junie laughs. "The water's fine with me. And can I have the nachos, please?"

"Nachos? I brought you all the way from Omaha for nachos?"

She smiles at the waitress, and they look at each other with something like complete understanding. Like they have known each other for ages and I just butted in.

"I've never been to Omaha," Junie says to her, "but I bet they have perfectly fine nachos. Ah, what the hell. I'll have the *chicken* nachos."

"And I'll have the lobster roll," I say.

The waitress leaves, and Junie starts, like an incantation, "Omaha. O. Ma. Ha. Oma*ha*. O—"

"You won't like it there," I say.

"You've been to Omaha?"

"No."

Awkward silence.

The nachos and lobster roll arrive quickly, and they are probably the finest in their respective fields. June refuses to even look at my food but kindly offers me samplings of hers. Excellent stuff, and I'm glad she got what she wanted rather than what I wanted her to want. A stunning sleek boat comes gliding in to dock close to where we are eating, and this, I realize, is our harbor cruise. It goes through the channel, a little way up the river into the city, then back out and around the harbor islands before coming back to dock in a couple of hours. I figure the views alone are going to be worth it. I get all excited, bursting to tell her.

"Isn't it stunning," I say about the boat, hoping I'm not overselling.

"Isn't it, though," she says dreamily, or sleepily.

It's getting near time. The scores of extremely happy-looking customers start to disembark. Then there's a crew already on the dock with cases of goodies for immediate restocking. We have hit things just right, as it seems like half the boaters are unloading straight into our cozy bar restaurant. We would never have gotten this table if we'd been just a little later.

"I ran into a friend of yours this afternoon," I say, full of confidence and pride at the way things are working out. Today, anyway, but today is what I have.

"Who's that?"

"One Who Knows," I say, big grin, big joke.

All expression slides right down her face, onto the floor, down the pier, into the Atlantic.

"You ran into him."

"Yeah, when I was running around, doing stuff, while you were working."

Her nostrils go wide, like a seal breaking the surface of the water.

"He's no fan of Ronny, apparently."

"Everyone hates my father. He's the great unifier. Brings all peoples together. Juan likes to pay him for the disgusting flunky jobs, and give him just enough to make sure he remains forever a disgusting flunky. Pays the bills. Pays no respect."

"Yeah. Well, anyway, I have to say I didn't find Juan as loathsome as I expected to. Almost likeable, really, in a face-of-evil way."

I suddenly become aware, probably should have done so before this, of Junie tensing up and wearing down simultaneously. It was a mistake. I stretched it too far, this feeling, this whatever. I should have kept it to myself, at least for now. She doesn't want to hear about this man, and I don't want her to hear about this man. Because of all that comes with it. Because of all that goes away with it.

"Anyway," I say too sharply as I receive the check, "I don't think you need to worry about him anymore."

She freezes me. I am looking down at the check, and I feel her glare, like a fishhook in my nose pulling me up to look at her.

"I didn't need to worry about him before," she says coldly.

"Right," I say, hurrying to sort out the bill and get away. "Well, okay. I guess I don't have to worry about him, then. After talking to him I feel less nervous, even if you never—"

"Did you do something you shouldn't have done, O?"

That feels, as soon as it lands, like the most profound question anyone has ever asked me.

"Nope," I say.

I have placed the bill on the table, and as we stare intensely at each other over it, it must look to other diners like a battle is about to commence over money.

"Good," she says.

My heart starts again, which is also good.

"Can we walk a little, up the pier?" I say, maneuvering things like I do it all the time. "Get a little stroll in and a good look at the boat at the same time?"

She shrugs, which I choose to take as enthusiasm.

We are walking alongside the big, gorgeous gleaming watercraft for which we have tickets, which she still does not know. We are holding hands. Junie is leaning on my shoulder heavily, even though she is not a leaner at all.

"I have another confession," she says softly.

"I love these," I say.

"I've never been on one of those things either." She is looking up at the boat with what looks like curiosity.

I don't know what the hotel charges for the total cosmic manipulation they are engineering on my behalf, but it's not enough.

"Would you like to?"

"No," she says without the malice of the lobster refusal. "I'm really tired."

"Come on. How tired could you be?"

"Well, I work really hard. And to be brutally frank, you do not."

And then sometimes the word "brutal" seems woefully insufficient.

"Game, set, and match," I say, bowing to her.

"See, you even speak tennis."

She makes me laugh even as she eviscerates me, which is itself impressive. "But you know it would be so—"

"It absolutely would," she says. "And I wouldn't enjoy one minute, O. I'm exhausted, beat, flat, and distracted. You know what I would really like? What would make this memorable, crazy little vacation end on a perfect note?"

"I'm all ears." Well, not *all* . . .

"I'd like to go up to our incredible room, smelling of flowers, fall down with you in our big crazy bed, and just lie there together, in front of the TV, in front of the gigantic window with the view, and just fall asleep together."

We stop just short of where the white-uniformed crewman is taking people's tickets and ushering them up the little gangway onto the boat.

Without hesitation or regret I steer to starboard, heading us back to port, to hotel, to all that Junie Blue just laid out.

On the way we skirt right past our table, where an older couple, maybe in their thirties, are sharing a pitcher of red beer. I take the cruise ticket out of my back pocket and slyly slap it onto the table between them.

Just as we are entering the hotel, I turn back to see them standing, draining beers, and scrambling seaward.

The night, I am thrilled to observe, goes the way Junie presented it, to the letter.

Except we do not fall asleep together. I linger for at least three more hours, leaning into her, breathing her, holding her, absorbing her, keeping her.

T e n

When I wake up, she is already gone.

There is a note, on hotel stationery, right next to me in the empty Junie space.

> *You looked so sweet. So serene.*
> *Had to work very early. Took the train.*
> *Lots to say, O. About all this.*
> *But there are no words.*
> *Love,*
> *J*

That is a word. Love. "Love" is definitely a word, and I'm hanging on to it.

I gather up my small bag of belongings. Then I go to the bath and collect all those ingredients that went into creating that once-in-a-lifetime Junie Blue mist in here last night. I have them now, for keeps.

Several of the roses are gone, and I throw several more into my bag before backing out of the room, looking it over and over, every inch, until the door shuts in front of me.

A short time later my good friends of the hotel have sorted me out, brought me my car, and sent me on my way, when my phone makes the new-message noise. I stop the car, having gotten only ten yards from the hotel front door.

Goddamn you, O, get down to the shop right now.

It is from my one true love. Her notes have a frightening mood swing quality to them today. Ominous, even.

When I enter—with great trepidation—the shop, Junie is behind the counter. One Who Knows/Juan Junose/Harry is standing just this side of the counter, with his horrible little dog panting away at his side.

"What does he mean, my obligation is cleared?" she yells at me. "Huh? What does he mean by that?"

There is very little room for me to maneuver here. So I don't.

"I'd say it means your obligation is cleared, June."

"Except that I never *had* an obligation to this man." She walks around the counter and stomps in my direction. "And if I did have an obligation, that obligation would be *mine* to deal with." When she reaches me, she starts punctuating every word with a sharp poke very high up in the middle of my chest. "I do not need to be taken care of by anybody. Do you understand me, you arrogant posh prick."

"That hurts, Junie," I say.

"Ah, women," Juan says, sounding very much like a man who desires a vicious chest poking.

"Women, is right, ya pig," she says.

"The last thing you need is to be mixed up in any way with dirty money," I say to her. "And now you're not. So that's a good thing."

I believe we have somehow made Juan's day, because he starts for the door with a deeply satisfied smile on his face. It's not enough, apparently, to win in whatever competition the likes of him are in. He has to create chaos in the lives of others to ice that cake properly.

"My money is not dirty," he says as he reaches me. "I employ the finest of financial consultants to see to that."

I get a shock right through me. It shoots up from my guts and certainly splashes all over my expression.

"*That's* what I was waiting to see," he says, pointing at my face before going on his way.

What was that? What did he say? Head games. I have had very little interaction with this man, but I have learned one thing quickly, and that is that his primary business is in head games.

"What was that he said?" I say to Junie after he's gone. "Did you hear that?"

"Get. Out," she says.

"Junie, listen. We have to talk—"

"We do not have to talk. If you don't get out of this store right now, I'm gonna call the cops, or the other guys, and tell them you're robbing the place. And that won't go well for you."

"Junie, please—"

"I mean it," she shouts, eyes closed, phone poised.

I go.

"I am *nobody's* bitch," she yells at my sorry, sorry, stupid back.

Eleven

It is over now. Yes, I am a numbskull for taking it this far before being able to make that statement. I have tried my calls and my texts and my stakeouts of dog walking routes. I have traveled near, though not into, her store. I have tried calling Maxie, but I get nowhere there, either. Mom talks to Leona, but nobody talks about Junie, at least not to me. Instructions are obviously in place. And a person has to be a certifiable lunatic to cross Junie Blue.

Yes, hello.

I haven't done much talking at all since Junie took my voice away.

I really thought I was doing something good there. And maybe that's what she means about the gulf between us.

I ache with every breath. Like all my ribs are broken, and stabbing my vital organs in the bargain.

Sunday comes, and I realize I haven't had a single conversation with my father for days. Way more than days. Way beyond days.

I think about the deal I made. I get more queasy every

hour I get closer to starting work. I start Monday.

Sunday sacreds.

The beach is mobbed, and I don't like it. It's an absolutely made-to-order call-it-up-from-room-service sunny summer Sunday. Kids and seagulls are squealing, indistinguishable. Dogs are not supposed to be on the beach. They're all here, all of them. My father and I are walking straight into the sun, along through the shallows, both of us in long pants—I don't know why, with the cuffs rolled insufficiently up.

"You're very quiet," he says, raising his voice to be heard over the waves and the music and the wildlife.

"I noticed that myself," I say. A Frisbee hits the water about a foot in front of me and splashes. I stare at it until a girl comes over to claim it.

"Sorry," she says.

Girls in inappropriate turquoise bikinis who have every business wearing them do not need to apologize, so the gesture is appreciated.

"Not a problem," I say, and she is gone.

"You know," Dad says as we resume our very stiff-legged bankers-go-beaching walk, "not that you necessarily need my coaching, but that looked like a missed opportunity to stretch your social muscles a bit."

"You think?" I say, looking back in the young lady's general direction.

"I do. Just, something you might want to keep in mind, openness to new experiences and opportunities."

"Ah," I say, sounding a little like a bitter and pissy and ungrateful teenager, "but that's what tomorrow's all about. We don't want to be overloading my circuits with too much all at once."

We are walking a greater distance than usual. We are approaching the stretch where the ridiculously beach-blanket-friendly white sand of the public beach starts giving way to the rugged boulder-strewn private one. The population and commotion drop off precipitously here, which is a welcome thing.

"That would be ambivalence about the next, exciting stage of your life I'm hearing?"

At this point farther progress requires some rock climbing, which I have always loved but Dad never showed much interest in. The tide is coming in and is just starting to slosh around in the gullies between the boulders. This is prime crabbing territory. We did a lot of rock-pool adventuring when I was a kid. Probably the single most durable and treasured component to our early-years experience. It was the original Communion of our Sunday sacreds.

"Sorry, Dad. I'm sure it will be great."

"I, myself, am certain of it," he says.

He scrabbles kind of awkwardly, up a rock that's about seven feet tall and five feet in circumference. He looks very much like a crab trying to climb a tree. That rock has got a twin, slightly shorter, six feet away, which I mount. We squat on our little mountains, me sitting like a chimp when gawking back at zoo patrons, him still crablike.

"I could release you from your obligation, if you feel this pessimistic, Son."

"No, Dad, you can't."

The waves are slapping at our rocks, the tide seeming to accelerate. He reaches into his breast pocket, because of course we have breast pockets at the beach.

"You did not have to do this," he says, holding out the check I wrote to Harry.

Is it possible to have a feeling, a reaction to something, and not have any idea what it is, even though it is going on inside your own body?

I do not know if I am surprised by this. I do not know if I am angry, or worried, or intrigued.

"I did what I had to do, Dad. I knew, at the time I did it, that I had to do exactly that. I knew it the way you know when you are hungry and have to eat."

He nods, and I know this smile-nod. It's his low-grade pride reaction when I say or do something that's not exactly monumental but that signals there is perhaps an active bio-culture of sorts existing inside me. The check continues to flutter like a flag.

"You should put that away before it flies," I say.

"Okay," he says. "But just so you know, this does not have to happen."

"It absolutely does."

"Well, you have impressed the man, at any rate. He wants no more from you. This finishes it."

I say nothing.

"You are an honorable man, Son."

"You work for him," I state flatly.

"He is a client."

"What do you do for him?"

"Same as I do for all my clients. I look out for his interests."

I look down at the slapping, splashing water reaching up for us.

"Do you do things you shouldn't do?"

This is most definitely not what my father expected of his Sunday sacreds. I do not know what he did expect, but I can read that it was nothing like this.

"Oliver, you know what I do, very simply? I do what's necessary. That, young man, is the same thing every single person who makes it in this world ultimately does. I do what needs to be done, to get by, to succeed, to provide for my family, and you have to admit I have done a pretty fair job of that over the years. Right?"

"No argument there."

"And in my business—probably in most businesses, but certainly in mine—there are decisions that need to be made every single day, hard ones, that not everybody is going to agree with. I do my best, make the tough calls, and at the end of it all I am certain that I am doing more good in this world than bad. And that, combined with success, is a pretty fair marker of a man's ledger in this life."

I am looking down now more than I am looking up. But I am listening.

"Are you listening?"

"I am."

"Does this make any sense to you? Do you appreciate where I am coming from?"

"I'm pretty sure I do, Dad."

"I hope so, O, I sure do. And I am confident, once you start making your way through this game, once you start connecting all the dots, once you appreciate all the things that a man's just got to do in certain situations, which I know you are going to click on—"

"As your shadow."

"As my shadow, exactly. Once all that starts falling in, once you see the world up close and for real, how the gears work and how guys like you and I *work* them . . . Well, I just know you are going to *get it*. You are going to get it, get it all, and get it like nobody's business. I just know it."

He is visibly excited. There is something primal about

what I'm seeing, elemental with the tide coming up to meet him and his mad pleasure barely contained.

He truly believes that that is going to happen. That I am going to be that man.

And, to my horror, I believe him too.

"And it all starts tomorrow morning," I shout, standing tall on my rock.

"Yes," he says, still squatting, still as always a bit more timid than I am about such stuff.

"I'll see you later, Dad," I say.

He's shouting something as I dive off the rock, in the direction of the open ocean.

Twelve

My suit, my bespoke gunmetal gray, summer-
weight fine wool suit fits me better than my actual flesh
does. I am a shark, I'm a blade, I am any number of beautiful
streamlined lethal things, and I honestly feel like I can do
what needs to be done, whatever needs to be done, in this
suit. I look in the full-length mirror hanging on the inside of
my closet door, and I'm stunned and intimidated by the trans-
formation. I would buy anything from this guy in the mirror.
I would do anything this guy told me to do, yes, including
dropping to my knees and blowing him.

Power.

I could also quite happily shoot him.

I sit at the breakfast table with Mom and Dad for the
first time this summer. Dad and I are, obviously, on the same
schedule now, but Mom is here for reasons known only to
herself. She usually likes to ease slowly into the day, a brief
kitchen cameo before taking coffee and laptop back to bed.
But here she is, staring at me with a mix of puzzlement and
sadness that is making me heartsick, for her.

Dad just looks up at me occasionally over his *Journal* and juice, keeping words to a minimum, for fear, I believe, of sideswiping whatever momentum I have for getting to that first day at the office. It's unspoken, but there is still enough of the same wiring in both of us that I believe we are both humming on this same wave—that somehow something irrevocable happens if we just get me across that threshold of day one of Shadow.

I would bet anything we're right about that. I believe there are *crossover* points, and this is one.

Looking at Mom, I would bet she would make that same bet.

She looks like she's at a wake. I feel like I am at a wake. Except, even at a wake people talk, a little.

The atmosphere is so spooky still that two of the three of us jump when my phone beeps a new message alert.

Put your makeup on, fix your hair up pretty, and meet me outside at seven thirty.

I check the time on the phone. Seven thirty-three.

"Excuse me," I say, nearly tipping my chair over backward as I fly for the door. I burst outside.

"Holy mother," I say.

"Holy mother right back atcha," she says.

Junie Blue is sitting there, parked right in front of my house, in the 1963 cobalt-blue Corvette that has been sitting in marquee position in the front lot of the classic-car dealer for the last three months. I have lusted secretly for this car every single day but feared if I spoke up, someone would buy it for me.

"Junie . . . wow."

"O . . . wow. I heard, through the grapevine—cough! LeonaMaxie—that you were walking the green mile in your monkey suit, but I didn't believe it."

I look down at my sharp-suited self.

"I only half-believe it myself."

"Even half is probably too much."

"I knew you wouldn't leave without me," I say. I knew nothing of the kind, so it must be the suit talking.

"Well, wrong again. I did leave without you, O. I got away, to the edge of town and beyond."

"But you came back. This is good. This is good. You'll give it another—"

"Wrong."

"Then what are you back for?"

She unfurls the most kill-me-dead-run-me-over-then-back-over-me-again-for-good-measure victorious Creamsicle smile the world could possibly stand.

"For you. For you. I came for you. Know why?"

I'm just conversing politely now, because why should I care why? "Why?"

"Because you need me. This is *me* rescuing *you*. From the horrors of what you were about to do. Me, saving you. And y'know, it feels kinda nice."

She guns and guns the great growly 'Vette engine.

"I can't really linger, O, so if you're coming . . ."

There is no rational debate to be had here—no emotional one, either for that matter. But I freeze up. This is huge and drastic and wild and way outside anything I even contemplated before, and without a doubt the exact opposite of what I was just about to do with myself this odd fine morning. I actually start lurching in the direction of the house.

"What are you doing?"

"Um, I don't know. I'll have to get . . . stuff."

She reaches across and throws the door open. "All the *stuff* you're ever gonna need is in here already."

And that has the effect of paralyzing me even further. I am stuck, like a frozen dopesicle, on the step.

"For the love of God, go!" Mom's wonderful, weird, warm voice groans at me from the front-room screen. "I will carry you to the car myself if I have to."

And that snaps it.

I run, jump into that fine automobile, driven by that fine woman, and we peel away, me waving crazily back at my mother, who is curdling the whole neighborhood with a cowboy howl I never knew she had.

. . .

We could not have gotten to open road faster if we'd taken a helicopter. The car loves the highway, and purrs to tell us so.

"So," I say, "where'd you get the money for this?"

"Walkin' . . . the . . . dogs," she drawls, the three words taking thirty minutes to come out.

I take my tie off and let it trail like our flag out the window.

"You know what is the one great thing that makes us right, Sweet Junie Blue Lies?"

"What is that one great thing, Lyin' O'Brien?"

"At least we lie to each other honestly."

She nods, considers, changes lanes without signaling.

"We would," she says, "if we ever lied."

I set the necktie free in the world that's now behind us.

"Ah. True," I say.

"True," she says.

True.